THE DALKEY ARCHIVE

THE DALKEY ARCHIVE

FLANN O'BRIEN

GRAFTON BOOKS

A Division of the Collins Publishing Group

LONDON GLASGOW
TORONTO SYDNEY AUCKLAND

Grafton Books
A Division of the Collins Publishing Group
8 Grafton Street, London W1X 3LA

First published in Great Britain 1964 by
MacGibbon & Kee Ltd
This edition published by Grafton Books 1986
Reprinted 1989

Copyright © Brian O'Nolan 1964

British Library Cataloguing in Publication Data

O'Brien, Flann
  The Dalkey archive.
  Rn: Brian O'Nolan   I. Title
  823'.912[F]   PR6029.N56

ISBN 0-246-12971-9

Printed in Great Britain by
St Edmundsbury Press, Bury St Edmunds, Suffolk

I dedicate these pages
to my Guardian Angel,
impressing upon him
that I'm only fooling
and warning him
to see to it that
there is no misunderstanding
when I go home.

I

Dalkey is a little town maybe twelve miles south of Dublin, on the shore. It is an unlikely town, huddled, quiet, pretending to be asleep. Its streets are narrow, not quite self-evident as streets and with meetings which seem accidental. Small shops look closed but are open. Dalkey looks like an humble settlement which must, a traveller feels, be next door to some place of the first importance and distinction. And it is – vestibule of a heavenly conspection.

Behold it. Ascend a shaded, dull, lane-like way, *per iter*, as it were, *tenebricosum*, and see it burst upon you as if a curtain had been miraculously whisked away. Yes, the Vico Road.

Good Lord!

The road itself curves gently upward and over a low wall to the left by the footpath enchantment is spread – rocky grassland falling fast away to reach a toy-like railway far below, with beyond it the immeasurable immanent sea, quietly moving slowly in the immense expanse of Killiney Bay. High in the sky which joins it at a seam far from precise, a caravan of light cloud labours silently to the east.

And to the right? Monstrous arrogance: a mighty shoulder of granite climbing ever away, its overcoat of furze and bracken embedded with stern ranks of pine, spruce, fir and horse-chestnut, with further on fine clusters of slim, meticulous eucalyptus – the whole a dazzle of mildly moving leaves, a farrago of light, colour, haze and copious air, a wonder that is quite vert, verdant, vertical, verticillate, vertiginous, in the shade of branches even vespertine. Heavens, has something escaped from the lexicon of Sergeant Fottrell?

But why this name Vico Road? Is there to be recalled in this magnificence a certain philosopher's pattern of man's lot on earth – thesis, antithesis, synthesis, chaos? Hardly. And is this to be compared with the Bay of Naples? That is not to be thought of, for in Naples there must be heat and hardness belabouring desiccated Italians – no soft Irish skies, no little breezes that feel almost coloured.

At a great distance ahead and up, one could see a remote little obelisk surmounting some steps where one can sit and contemplate all this scene: the sea, the peninsula of Howth across the bay and distantly, to the right, the dim outline of the Wicklow mountains, blue or grey. Was the monument erected to honour the Creator of all this splendour? No. Perhaps in remembrance of a fine Irish person He once made – Johannes Scotus Erigena, perhaps, or possibly Parnell? No indeed: Queen Victoria.

Mary was nudging Michael Shaughnessy. She loitered enticingly about the fringes of his mind; the deep brown eyes, the light hair, the gentleness yet the poise. She was really a nuisance yet never far away. He frowned and closed his fist, but intermittent muttering immediately behind him betokened that Hackett was there.

– How is she getting on, he asked, drawing level, that pious Mary of yours?

It was by no means the first time that this handsome lout had shown his ability to divine thought, a nasty gift.

– Mind your own business, Shaugnessy said sourly. I never ask about the lady you call Asterisk Agnes.

– If you want to know, she's very well, thank you.

They walked in, loosely clutching their damp bathing things.

In the low seaward wall there was a tiny gap which gave access to a rough downhill path towards the railway far below; there a footbridge led to a bathing place called White Rock. At this gap a man was standing, supporting himself somewhat with a hand on the wall. As Shaughnessy drew near he saw the man was spare, tall, clean-shaven, with sparse fairish hair combed sideways across an oversize head.

– This poor bugger's hurt, Hackett remarked.

The man's face was placid and urbane but contorted in a slight grimace. He was wearing sandals and his right foot in the region of the big toe was covered with fresh blood. They stopped.

– Are you hurt, sir? Hackett asked.

The man politely examined each of them in turn.

– I suppose I am, he replied. There are notices down there about the dangers of the sea. Usually there is far more danger on land. I bashed my right toes on a sharp little dagger of granite I didn't see on that damned path.

– Perhaps we could help, Shaughnessy said. We'd be happy to assist you down to the Colza Hotel in Dalkey. We could get you a chemist there or maybe a doctor.

The man smiled slightly.

– That's good of you, he replied, but I'm my own doctor. Perhaps though you could give me a hand to get home?

– Well, certainly, Shaughnessy said.

– Do you live far, sir? Hackett asked.

– Just up there, the man said, pointing to the towering trees. It's a stiff climb with a cut foot.

Shaughnessy had no idea that there was any house in the fastness pointed to, but almost opposite there was a tiny gate discernible in the rough railing bounding the road.

– So long as you're sure there *is* a house there, Hackett said brightly, we will be honoured to be of valuable succour.

– The merit of the house is that hardly anybody except the postman knows it's there, the other replied agreeably.

They crossed the road, the two escorts lightly assisting at each elbow. Inside the gate a narrow but smooth enough pathway fastidiously picked its way upward through tree-trunks and shrubs.

– Might as well introduce myself, the invalid said. My name's De Selby.

Shaughnessy gave his, adding that everybody called him Mick. He noticed that Hackett styled himself just Mr Hack-

9

ett: it seemed an attitude of polite neutrality, perhaps condescension.

– This part of the country, De Selby remarked, is
surprisingly full of tinkers, gawms and gobshites. Are you
gentlemen skilled in the Irish language?

The non-sequitur rather took Shaughnessy aback, but not
Hackett.

– I know a great lot about it, sir. A beautiful tongue.

– Well, the word *mór* means big. In front of my house –
we're near it now – there is a lawn surprisingly large considering the terrain. I thought I would combine *mór* and
lawn as a name for the house. A hybrid, of course, but what
matter? I found a looderamawn in Dalkey village by the
name of Teague McGettigan. He's the local cabman, handy-
man, and observer of the weather; there is absolutely
nothing he can't do. I asked him to paint the name on the
gate, and told him the words. Now wait till you see the result.

The house could now be glimpsed, a low villa of timber
and brick. As they drew nearer De Selby's lawn looked big
enough but regrettably it was a sloping expanse of coarse,
scruffy grass embroidered with flat weeds. And in black
letters on the wooden gate was the title: LAWNMOWER.
Shaughnessy and Hackett sniggered as De Selby sighed elab-
orately.

– Well the dear knows I always felt that Teague was our
domestic Leonardo, Hackett chuckled. I'm well acquainted
with the poor bastard.

They sidled gently inward. De Selby's foot was now dirty
as well as bloody.

2

Our mutilated friend seems a decent sort of segotia, Hackett remarked from his armchair. De Selby had excused himself while he attended to 'the medication of my pedal pollex', and the visitors gazed about his living room with curiosity. It was oblong in shape, spacious, with a low ceiling. Varnished panelling to the height of about eighteen inches ran right round the walls, which otherwise bore faded greenish paper. There were no pictures. Two heavy mahogany bookcases, very full, stood in embrasures to each side of the fireplace, with a large press at the blank end of the room. There were many chairs, a small table in the centre and by the far wall a biggish table bearing sundry scientific instruments and tools, including a microscope. What looked like a powerful lamp hovered over this and to the left was an upright piano by Liehr, with music on the rest. It was clearly a bachelor's apartment but clean and orderly. Was he perhaps a musician, a medical man, a theopneust, a geodetic chemist ... a savant?

– He's snug here anyway, Mick Shaughnessy said, and very well hidden away.

– He's the sort of man, Hackett replied, that could be up to any game at all in this sort of secret H.Q. He might be a dangerous character.

Soon De Selby re-appeared, beaming, and took his place in the centre, standing with his back to the empty fireplace.

– A superficial vascular lesion, he remarked pleasantly, now cleansed, disinfected, anointed, and with a dressing you see which is impenetrable even by water.

– You mean, you intend to continue swimming? Hackett asked.

– Certainly.

– Bravo! Good man.

– Oh not at all – it's part of my business. By the way, would it be rude to enquire what is the business of you gentlemen?

– I'm a lowly civil servant, Mick replied. I detest the job, its low atmosphere and the scruff who are my companions in the office.

– I'm worse off, Hackett said in mock sorrow. I work for the father, who's a jeweller but a man that's very careful with the keys. No opportunity of giving myself an increase in pay. I suppose you could call me a jeweller too, or perhaps a sub-jeweller. Or a paste jeweller.

– Very interesting work, for I know a little about it. Do you cut stones?

– Sometimes.

– Yes. Well I'm a theologist and a physicist, sciences which embrace many others such as eschatology and astrognosy. The peace of this part of the world makes true thinking possible. I think my researches are nearly at an end. But let me entertain you for a moment.

He sat down at the piano and after some slow phrases, erupted into what Mick with inward wit, would dub a head-long chromatic dysentery which was 'brilliant' in the bad sense of being inchoate and, to his ear at least, incoherent. A shattering chord brought the disorder to a close.

– Well, he said, rising, what did you think of that?

Hackett looked wise.

– I think I detected Liszt in one of his less guarded moments, he said.

– No, De Selby answered. The basis of that was the canon at the start of César Franck's well-known sonata for violin and piano. The rest was all improvisation. By me.

– You're a splendid player, Mick ventured archly.

– It's only for amusement but a piano can be a very useful instrument. Wait till I show you something.

He returned to the instrument, lifted half of the hinged top and took out a bottle of yellowish liquid, which he placed on the table. Then opening a door in the nether part of a bookcase, he took out three handsome stem glasses and a decanter of what looked like water.

– This is the best whiskey to be had in Ireland, faultlessly made and perfectly matured. I know you will not refuse a taiscaun.

– Nothing would make me happier, Hackett said. I notice that there's no label on the bottle.

– Thank you, Mick said, accepting a generous glass from De Selby. He did not like whiskey much, or any intoxicant, for that matter. But manners came first. Hackett followed his example.

– The water's there, De Selby gestured. Don't steal another man's wife and never water his whiskey. No label on the bottle? True. I made that whiskey myself.

Hackett had taken a tentative sip.

– I hope you know that whiskey doesn't mature in a bottle. Though I must say that this tastes good.

Mick and De Selby took a reasonable gulp together.

– My dear fellow, De Selby replied, I know all about sherry casks, temperature, subterranean repositories and all that extravaganza. But such considerations do not arise here. This whiskey was made last week.

Hackett leaned forward in his chair, startled.

– What was that? he cried. A week old? Then it can't be whiskey at all. Good God, are you trying to give us heart failure or dissolve our kidneys?

De Selby's air was one of banter.

– You can see, Mr Hackett, that I am also drinking this excellent potion myself. And I did not say it was a week old. I said it was made last week.

– Well, this is Saturday. We needn't argue about a day or two.

– Mr De Selby, Mick interposed mildly, it is clear enough that you are making some distinction in what you said, that there is some nicety of terminology in your words. I can't quite follow you.

De Selby here took a drink which may be described as profound and then suddenly an expression of apocalyptic solemnity came over all his mild face.

– Gentlemen, he said, in an empty voice, I have mastered time. Time has been called, an event, a repository, a continuum, an ingredient of the universe. I can suspend time, negative its apparent course.

Mick thought it funny in retrospect that Hackett here glanced at his watch, perhaps involuntarily.

– Time is still passing with me, he croaked.

– The passage of time, De Selby continued, is calculated with reference to the movements of the heavenly bodies. These are fallacious as determinants of the nature of time. Time has been studied and pronounced upon by many apparently sober men – Newton, Spinoza, Bergson, even Descartes. The postulates of the Relativity nonsense of Einstein are mendacious, not to say bogus. He tried to say that time and space had no real existence separately but were to be apprehended only in unison. Such pursuits as astronomy and geodesy have simply befuddled man. You understand?

As it was at Mick he looked the latter firmly shook his head but thought well to take another stern sup of whiskey. Hackett was frowning. De Selby sat down by the table.

– Consideration of time, he said, from intellectual, philosophic or even mathematical criteria is fatuity, and the preoccupation of slovens. In such unseemly brawls some priestly fop is bound to induce a sort of cerebral catalepsy by bringing forward terms such as infinity and eternity.

Mick thought it seemly to say something, however foolish.

– If time is illusory as you seem to suggest, Mr De Selby, how is it that when a child is born, with time he grows to be a boy, then a man, next an old man and finally a spent and helpless cripple?

De Selby's slight smile showed a return of the benign mood.

– There you have another error in formulating thought.

14

You confound time with organic evolution. Take your child who has grown to be a man of twenty-one. His total life-span is to be seventy years. He has a horse whose life-span is to be twenty. He goes for a ride on his horse. Do these two creatures subsist simultaneously in dissimilar conditions of time? Is the velocity of time for the horse three and a half times that for the man?

Hackett was now alert.

– Come here, he said. That greedy fellow the pike is reputed to grow to be up to two hundred years of age. How is our time-ratio if he is caught and killed by a young fellow of fifteen?

– Work it out for yourself, De Selby replied pleasantly. Divergences, incompatibilities, irreconcilables are everywhere. Poor Descartes! He tried to reduce all goings-on in the natural world to a code of mechanics, kinetic but not dynamic. All motion of objects was circular, he denied a vacuum was possible and affirmed that weight existed irrespective of gravity. *Cogito ergo sum?* He might as well have written *inepsias scripsi ergo sum* and prove the same point, as *he* thought.

– That man's work, Mick interjected, may have been mistaken in some conclusions but was guided by his absolute belief in Almighty God.

– True indeed. I personally don't discount the existence of a supreme *supra mundum* power but I sometimes doubted if it is benign. Where are we with this mess of Cartesian methodology and Biblical myth-making? Eve, the snake and the apple. Good Lord!

– Give us another drink if you please, Hackett said. Whiskey is not incompatible with theology, particularly magic whiskey that is ancient and also a week old.

– Most certainly, said De Selby, rising and ministering most generously to the three glasses. He sighed as he sat down again.

– You men, he said, should read all the works of Descartes,

having first thoroughly learnt Latin. He is an excellent example of blind faith corrupting the intellect. He knew Galileo, of course, accepted the latter's support of the Copernican theory that the earth moves round the sun and had in fact been busy on a treatise affirming this. But when he heard that the Inquisition had condemned Galileo as a heretic, he hastily put away his manuscript. In our modern slang he was yellow. And his death was perfectly ridiculous. To ensure a crust for himself, he agreed to call on Queen Christina of Sweden three times a week at five in the morning to teach her philosophy. Five in the morning in that climate! It killed him, of course. Know what age he was?

Hackett had just lit a cigarette without offering one to anybody.

– I feel Descartes' head was a little bit loose, he remarked ponderously, not so much for his profusion of erroneous ideas but for the folly of a man of eighty-two thus getting up at such an unearthly hour and him near the North Pole.

– He was fifty-four, De Selby said evenly.

– Well by damn, Mick blurted, he was a remarkable man however crazy his scientific beliefs.

– There's a French term I heard which might describe him, Hackett said. *Idiot-savant.*

De Selby produced a solitary cigarette of his own and lit it. How had he inferred that Mick did not smoke?

– At worst, he said in a tone one might call oracular, Descartes was a solipsist. Another weakness of his was a liking for the Jesuits. He was very properly derided for regarding space as a plenum. It is a coincidence, of course, but I have made the parallel but undoubted discovery that *time* is a plenum.

– What does that mean? Hackett asked.

– One might describe a plenum as a phenomenon or existence full of itself but inert. Obviously space does not satisfy such a condition. But time is a plenum, immobile, immutable, ineluctable, irrevocable, a condition of absolute stasis.

Time does not pass. Change and movement may occur within time.

Mick pondered this. Comment seemed pointless. There seemed no little straw to clutch at; nothing to question.

– Mr De Selby, he ventured at last, it would seem impertinent of the like of me to offer criticism or even opinions on what I apprehend as purely abstract propositions. I'm afraid I harbour the traditional idea and experience of time. For instance, if you permit me to drink enough of this whiskey, by which I mean too much, I'm certain to undergo unmistakable temporal punishment. My stomach, liver and nervous system will be wrecked in the morning.

– To say nothing of the dry gawks, Hackett added.

De Selby laughed civilly.

– That would be a change to which time, of its nature, is quite irrelevant.

– Possibly, Hackett replied, but that academic observation will in no way mitigate the reality of the pain.

– A tincture, De Selby said, again rising with the bottle and once more adding generously to the three glasses. You must excuse me for a moment or two.

Needless to say, Hackett and Mick looked at each other in some wonder when he had left the room.

– This malt seems to be superb, Hackett observed, but would he have dope or something in it?

– Why should there be? He's drinking plenty of it himself.

– Maybe he's gone away to give himself a dose of some antidote. Or an emetic.

Mick shook his head genuinely.

– He's a strange bird, he said, but I don't think he's off his head, or a public danger.

– You're certain he's not derogatory?

– Yes. Call him eccentric.

Hackett rose and gave himself a hasty extra shot from the bottle, which in turn Mick repelled with a gesture. He lit another cigarette.

– Well, he said, I suppose we should not overstay our welcome. Perhaps we should go. What do you say?

Mick nodded. The experience had been curious and not to be regretted; and it could perhaps lead to other interesting things or even people. How commonplace, he reflected, were all the people he did know.

When De Selby returned he carried a tray with plates, knives, a dish of butter and an ornate basket full of what seemed golden bread.

– Sit in to the table, lads – pull over your chairs, he said. This is merely what the Church calls a collation. These delightful wheaten farls were made by me, like the whiskey, but you must not think I'm like an ancient Roman emperor living in daily fear of being poisoned. I'm alone here, and it's a long painful pilgrimage to the shops.

With a murmur of thanks the visitors started this modest and pleasant meal. De Selby himself took little and seemed preoccupied.

– Call me a theologian or a physicist as you will, he said at last rather earnestly, but I am serious and truthful. My discoveries concerning the nature of time were in fact quite accidental. The objective of my research was altogether different. My aim was utterly unconnected with the essence of time.

– Indeed? Hackett said rather coarsely as he coarsely munched. And what was the main aim?

– To destroy the whole world.

They stared at him. Hackett made a slight noise but De Selby's face was set, impassive, grim.

– Well, well, Mick stammered.

– It merits destruction. Its history and prehistory, even its present, is a foul record of pestilence, famine, war, devastation and misery so terrible and multifarious that its depth and horror are unknown to any one man. Rottenness is universally endemic, disease is paramount. The human race is finally debauched and aborted.

– Mr De Selby, Hackett said with a want of gravity, would it be rude to ask just how you will destroy the world? You did not make it.

– Even you, Mr Hackett, have destroyed things you did not make. I do not care a farthing about who made the world or what the grand intention was, laudable or horrible. The creation is loathsome and abominable, and total extinction could not be worse.

Mick could see that Hackett's attitude was provoking brusqueness whereas what was needed was elucidation. Even marginal exposition by De Selby would throw light on the important question – was he a true scientist or just demented?

– I can't see, sir, Mick ventured modestly, how this world could be destroyed short of arranging a celestial collision between it and some other great heavenly body. How a man could interfere with the movements of the stars – I find that an insoluble puzzle, sir.

De Selby's taut expression relaxed somewhat.

– Since our repast is finished, have another drink, he said, pushing forward the bottle. When I mentioned destroying the whole world, I was not referring to the physical planet but to every manner and manifestation of life on it. When my task is accomplished – and I feel that will be soon – nothing living, not even a blade of grass, a flea – will exist on this globe. Nor shall I exist myself, of course.

– And what about us? Hackett asked.

– You must participate in the destiny of all mankind, which is extermination.

– Guesswork is futile, Mr De Selby, Mick murmured, but could this plan of yours involve liquefying all the ice at the Poles and elsewhere and thus drowning everything, in the manner of the Flood in the Bible?

– No. The story of that Flood is just silly. We are told it was caused by a deluge of forty days and forty nights. All this water must have existed on earth before the rain started, for more can not come down than was taken up. Commonsense tells me that this is childish nonsense.

– That is merely a feeble rational quibble, Hackett cut in. He liked to show that he was alert.

– What then, sir, Mick asked in painful humility, is the secret, the supreme crucial secret?

De Selby gave a sort of grimace.

– It would be impossible for me, he explained, to give you gentlemen, who have no scientific training, even a glimpse into my studies and achievements in pneumatic chemistry. My work has taken up the best part of a life-time and, though assistance and co-operation were generously offered by men abroad, they could not master my fundamental postulate: namely, the annihilation of the atmosphere.

– You mean, abolish air? Hackett asked blankly.

– Only its biogenic and substantive ingredient, replied De Selby, which, of course, is oxygen.

– Thus, Mick interposed, if you extract all oxygen from the atmosphere or destroy it, all life will cease?

– Crudely put, perhaps, the scientist agreed, now again genial, but you may grasp the idea. There are certain possible complications but they need not trouble us now.

Hackett had quietly helped himself to another drink and showed active interest.

– I think I see it, he intoned. Exit automatically the oxygen and we have to carry on with what remains, which happens to be poison. Isn't it murder though?

De Selby paid no attention.

– The atmosphere of the earth, meaning what in practice we breathe as distinct from rarefied atmosphere at great heights, is composed of roughly 78 per cent nitrogen, 21 oxygen, tiny quantities of argon and carbon dioxide, and microscopic quantities of other gases such as helium and ozone. Our preoccupation is with nitrogen, atomic weight 14.008, atomic number 7.

– Is there a smell off nitrogen? Hackett enquired.

– No. After extreme study and experiment I have produced a chemical compound which totally eliminates oxygen from any given atmosphere. A minute quantity of this hard substance, small enough to be invisible to the naked eye, would thus convert the interior of the greatest hall on earth into a dead world provided, of course, the hall were properly sealed. Let me show you.

He quietly knelt at one of the lower presses and opened the door to reveal a small safe of conventional aspect. This he opened with a key, revealing a circular container of dull metal of a size that would contain perhaps four gallons of liquid. Inscribed on its face were the letters D.M.P.

– Good Lord, Hackett cried, the D.M.P.! The good old D.M.P.! The grandfather was a member of that bunch.

De Selby turned his head, smiling bleakly.

– Yes – the D.M.P. – the Dublin Metropolitan Police. My own father was a member. They are long-since abolished, of course.

– Well what's the idea of putting that on your jar of chemicals?

De Selby had closed the safe and press door and gone back to his seat.

– Just a whim of mine, no more, he replied. The letters are in no sense a formula or even a mnemonic. But that container has in it the most priceless substance on earth.

– Mr De Selby, Mick said, rather frightened by these flamboyant proceedings, granted that your safe is a good one, is it not foolish to leave such dangerous stuff here for some burglar to knock it off?

– Me, for instance? Hackett interposed.

– No, gentlemen, there is no danger at all. Nobody would know what the substance was, its properties or how activated.

– But don't *we* know? Hackett insisted.

– You know next to nothing, De Selby replied easily, but I intend to enlighten you even more.

– I assure you, Mick thought well to say, that any information entrusted to us will be treated in strict confidence.

– Oh, don't bother about that, De Selby said politely, it's not information I'll supply but experience. A discovery I have made – and quite unexpectedly – is that a de-oxygenated atmosphere cancels the apparently serial nature of time and confronts us with true time and simultaneously with all the things and creatures which time has ever contained or will contain, provided we evoke them. Do you follow? Let us be serious about this. The situation is momentous and scarcely of this world as we know it.

He stared at each of his two new friends in turn very gravely.

– I feel, he announced, that you are entitled to some personal explanation concerning myself. It would be quite wrong to regard me as a christophobe.

– Me too, Hackett chirped impudently.

– The early books of the Bible I accepted as myth, but durable myth contrived genuinely for man's guidance. I also accepted as fact the story of the awesome encounter between God and the rebel Lucifer. But I was undecided for many years as to the outcome of that encounter. I had little to corroborate the revelation that God had triumphed and banished Lucifer to hell forever. For if – I repeat *if* – the decision had gone the other way and God had been vanquished, who but Lucifer would be certain to put about the other and opposite story?

– But why should he? Mick asked incredulously.

– The better to snare and damn mankind, De Selby answered.

– Well now, Hackett remarked, that secret would take some keeping.

– However, De Selby continued, perplexed, I was quite mistaken in that speculation. I've since found that things are as set forth in the Bible, at least to the extent that heaven is intact.

Hackett gave a low whistle, perhaps in derision.

— How could you be sure? he asked. You have not been temporarily out of this world, have you, Mr De Selby?

— Not exactly. But I have had a long talk with John the Baptist. A most understanding man, do you know, you'd swear he was a Jesuit.

— Good heavens! Mick cried, while Hackett hastily put his glass on the table with a click.

— Ah yes, most understanding. Perfect manners, of course, and a courteous appreciation of my own personal limitations. A very *interesting* man the same Baptist.

— Where did this happen? Hackett asked.

— Here in Dalkey, De Selby explained. Under the sea.

There was a small but absolute silence.

— While time stood still? Hackett persisted.

— I'll bring both of you people to the same spot tomorrow. That is, if you wish it and provided you can swim, and for a short distance under water.

— We are both excellent swimmers, Hackett said cheerfully, except I'm by far the better of the pair.

— We'd be delighted, Mick interrupted with a sickly smile, on the understanding that we'll get safely back.

— There is no danger whatever. Down at the headquarters of the Vico Swimming Club there is a peculiar chamber hidden in the rocks at the water's edge. At low tide there is cavernous access from the water to this chamber. As the tide rises this hole is blocked and air sealed off in the chamber. The water provides a total seal.

— This could be a chamber of horrors, Hackett suggested.

— I have some masks of my own design, equipped with compressed air, normal air, and having an automatic feed-valve. The masks and tank are quite light, of aluminium.

— I think I grasp the idea, Mick said in a frown of concentration. We go under the water wearing these breathing gadgets, make our way through this rocky opening to the chamber, and there meet John the Baptist?

23

De Selby chuckled softly.

– Not necessarily and not quite. We get to the empty chamber as you say and I then release a minute quantity of D.M.P. We are then subsisting in timeless nitrogen but still able to breathe from the tanks on our backs.

– Does our physical weight change? Hackett asked.

– Yes, somewhat.

– And what happens then?

– We shall see what happens after you have met me at this swimming pool at eight o'clock tomorrow morning. Are you going back by the Colza Hotel?

– Certainly.

– Well have a message sent to Teague McGettigan to call for me with his damned cab at 7.30. Those mask affairs are bothersome to horse about with.

Thus the appointment was made. De Selby affable as he led his visitors to his door and said goodbye.

3 _____

Hackett was frowning a bit and taciturn as the two strolled down the Vico Road towards Dalkey. Mick felt preoccupied, his ideas in some disarray. Some light seemed to have been drained from the sunny evening.

– We don't often have this sort of diversion, Hackett, he remarked.

– It certainly isn't every day we're offered miraculous whiskey, Hackett answered gloomily, and told at the same time we're under sentence of death. Shouldn't other people be warned? Our personal squaws, for instance?

– That would be what used to be called spreading despondency and disaffection, Mick warned pompously. What good would it do?

– They could go to confession, couldn't they?

– So could you. But the people would only laugh at us. So far as you are concerned, they'd say you were drunk.

– That week-old gargle was marvellous stuff, he muttered reflectively after a pause. I feel all right but I'm still not certain that there wasn't some sort of a drug in it. Slow-acting hypnotic stuff, or something worse that goes straight to the brain. We might yet go berserk by the time we reach the Colza. Maybe we'll be arrested by Sergeant Fottrell.

– Divil a fear of it.

– I certainly wouldn't like to swear the truth of today in court.

– We have an appointment early tomorrow morning, Mick reminded him. I suggest we say nothing to anybody about today's business.

– Do you intend to keep tomorrow's date?

– I certainly do. But I'll have to use the bike to get here from Booterstown at that hour.

They walked on, silent in thought.

It is not easy to give an account of the Colza Hotel, its owner Mrs Laverty, or its peculiar air. It had been formerly, though not in any recent time, an ordinary public house labelled 'Constantine Kerr, Licensed Vintner' and it was said that Mrs Laverty, a widow, had remodelled the bar, erased the obnoxious public house title and called the premises the Colza Hotel.

Why this strange name?

Mrs Laverty was a most religious woman and once had a talk with a neighbour about the red lamp suspended in the church before the high altar. When told it was sustained with colza oil, she piously assumed that this was a holy oil used for miraculous purposes by Saint Colza, V.M.*, and decided to put her house under this banner.

* Virgin Martyr.

Here is the layout of the bar in the days when Hackett and Shaughnessy were customers:

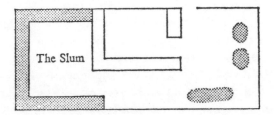

The area known as 'The Slum' was spacious with soft leather seating by the wall and other seats and small tables about the floor. Nobody took the hotel designation seriously, though Mrs Laverty stoutly held that there were 'many good beds' upstairs. A courageous stranger who demanded a meal would be given rashers and eggs in a desultory back kitchen. About the time now dealt with Mrs Laverty had been long saving towards a pilgrimage to Lourdes. Was she deaf? Nobody was sure. The doubt had arisen some years ago when Hackett openly addressed her as Mrs Lavatory, of which she never took any notice. Hard of hearing, perhaps, she may also have thought that Hackett had never been taught to speak properly.

When Hackett and Shaughnessy walked in after the De Selby visit, the 'Slum' or habitat of cronies was occupied by Dr Crewett, a very old and wizened and wise medical man who had seen much service in the R.A.M.C. but disdained to flaunt a military title. A strange young man was sitting near him and Mrs Laverty was seated behind the bar, knitting.

— Hello to all and thank God to be back in civilization, Hackett called. Mrs L, give me two glass skillets of your patent Irish malt, please.

She smiled perfunctorily in her large homely face and moved to obey. She did not like Hackett much.

— Where were ye? Dr Crewett asked.

— Walking, Mick said.

– You gents have been taking the intoxicating air, he observed. Your complexions do ye great credit.

– It has been a good day, doctor, Mick added civilly.

– We have been inhaling oxygen, theology and astral physics, Hackett said, accepting two glasses from Mrs Laverty.

– Ah, physics? I see, the young stranger said politely. He was slim, black-haired, callow, wore thick glasses and looked about nineteen.

– The Greek word *kinesis* should not be ignored, Hackett said learnedly but with an air of jeer.

– Hackett, Mick interjected in warning, I think it's better for us to mind our own business.

– It happens that I'm doing medicine at Trinity, the stranger added. I'm out here looking for digs.

– Why come out to this wilderness, Hackett asked, and have yourself trailing in and out of town every day?

– This is a new friend of ours, Dr Crewett explained. May I introduce Mr Nemo Crabbe?

Nods were exchanged and Hackett raised his glass in salute.

– If you mean take rooms in Trinity, Crabbe replied, no, thanks. They are vile, ramshackle quarters, and a resident student there is expected to empty his own charley.

– In my days in Egypt we hadn't even got such a thing. But there was limitless sand and wastes of scrub.

– Besides, Crabbe added, I like the sea.

– Well, fair enough, Hackett growled, why not stay right here. This is a hotel.

Mrs Laverty raised her head, displeased.

– I have already told the gentleman, Mr Hackett, she said sharply, that we're full up.

– Yes, but of what?

Dr Crewett, a peace-maker, intervened.

– Mrs Laverty, I think I'll buy a glawsheen all round if you would be so kind.

She nodded, mollified a bit, and rose.

– Damned physics and chemistry are for me a scourge, Crabbe confided to all. It's my father who insists on this medicine nonsense. I have no interest at all in it, and Dr Crewett agrees with my attitude.

– Certainly, the medico nodded.

– He believes that doctors of today are merely messenger boys for the drug firms.

– Lord, drugs, Hackett muttered.

– And very dangerous and untested drugs many of them are, Dr Crewett added.

– Nobody can take away Dr Glauber's great triumph, Hackett remarked, grasping his new drink. I've often wondered that since *glauben* means 'to think', whether *Glauber* means thinker? Remember the pensive attitude of the seated one.

– It doesn't, Mick said brusquely, for he had briefly studied German.

– Actually, poetry is my real interest, Crabbe said. I suppose I have something in common with Shelley and Byron. The sea, I mean, and poetry. The sea is a poem in itself.

– It has metre, too, Hackett's voice sneered. Nothing finer than a good breeze and a 12-metre boat out there in the bay.

Mrs Laverty's gentle voice was heard from her averted face.

– I'm very fond of poetry. That thing the Hound of Heaven is grand. As a girl I knew bits of it by heart.

– Some people think it's doggerel.

– I suppose, Crabbe ventured, that all you good friends think my Christian name is odd. Nemo.

– It *is* odd, Mick agreed in what was meant to be a kindly tone. And if I may say so, your father must be an odd man.

– It was my mother, I believe.

– You could always change it, Crabbe, Dr Crewett suggested. In common law a man can call himself and be known by any name he likes.

– That reminds me of the poor man whose surname was

Piss, Hackett recounted. He didn't like it and changed it by deed-poll to Vomit.

– I implore you not to be facetious, the unsmiling Crabbe replied. The funny thing is that I like the name Nemo. Try thinking of it backwards.

– Well, you have something there, Hackett granted.

– Poetic, what?

There was a short silence which Dr Crewett broke.

– That makes you think, he said thoughtfully. Wouldn't it be awful to have the Arab surname Esra?

– Let us have another round, Sussim L, Mick said facetiously, before I go home to beautiful Booterstown.

She smiled. She was fond of him in her own way. But had she heard his hasty transliteration? Hackett was scribbling a note.

– Mrs L, he said loudly, could you see that Teague McGettigan gets this tonight? It's about an urgent appointment with another man for tomorrow morning.

– I will, Mr Hackett.

They left soon afterwards, going homewards by tram. Hackett got off at Monkstown, not far away, where he lived.

Mick felt well enough, and wondered about the morrow. After all, De Selby had done nothing more than talk. Much of it was astonishing talk but he had promised actual business at an hour not so long after dawn. Assuming he turned up with his gear, was there risk? Would the unreliable Hackett be there?

He sighed. Time, even if there was no such thing, would tell.

4

Mild air with the sea in a stage whisper behind it was in Mick's face as his bicycle turned into the lane-like approach to the Vico Road and its rocky swimming hole. It was a fine morning, calm, full of late summer.

Teague McGettigan's cab was at the entrance, the horse's head submerged in a breakfast nose-bag. Mick went down the steps and saluted the company with a hail of his arm. De Selby was gazing in disfavour at a pullover he had just taken off. Hackett was slumped seated, fully dressed and smoking a cigarette, while McGettigan in his dirty raincoat was fastidiously attending to his pipe. De Selby nodded. Hackett muttered 'More luck' and McGettigan spat.

– Boys-a-dear, McGettigan said in a low voice from his old thin unshaven face, ye'll get the right drenching today. Ye'll be soaked to the pelt.

– Considering that we're soon to dive into that water, Hackett replied, I won't dispute your prophecy, Teague.

– I don't mean that. Look at that bloody sky.

– Cloudless, Mick remarked.

– For Christ's sake look down there by Wickla.

In that quarter there was what looked like sea-haze, with the merest hint of the great mountain behind. With his hands Mick made a gesture of nonchalance.

– We might be down under the water for half an hour, I believe, Hackett said, or at least that's Mr De Selby's story. We have an appointment with mermaids or something.

– Get into your togs, Hackett, De Selby said impatiently. And you, too, Mick.

– Ye'll pay more attention to me, Teague muttered, when ye come up to find ye'r superfine clothes demolished be the lashin rain.

– Can't you keep them in your cursed droshky? De Selby barked. His temper was clearly a bit uncertain.

All got ready. Teague sat philosophically on a ledge, smoking and having the air of an indulgent elder watching children at play. Maybe his attitude was justified. When the three were ready for the water De Selby beckoned them to private consultation. The gear was spread out on a flattish rock.

– Now listen carefully, he said. This apparatus I am going to fit on both of you allows you to breathe, under water or out of it. The valve is automatic and needs no adjustment, nor is that possible. The air is compressed and will last half an hour by conventional effluxion of time.

– Thank God, sir, that your theories about time are not involved in the air supply, Hackett remarked.

– The apparatus also allows you to hear. My own is somewhat different. It enables me to do all that but speak and be heard as well. Follow?

– That seems clear enough, Mick agreed.

– When I clip the masks in place your air supply is *on*, he said emphatically. Under water or on land you can breathe.

– Fair enough, Hackett said politely.

– And listen to this, De Selby continued, I will go first, leading the way, over there to the left, to this cave opening, now submerged. It is only a matter of yards and not deep down. The tide is now nearly full. Follow close behind me. When we get to the rock apartment, take a seat as best you can, do nothing, and wait. At first it will be dark but you won't be cold. I will then annihilate the terrestrial atmosphere and the time illusion by activating a particle of D.M.P. Now is all that clear? I don't want any attempt at technical guff or questions at this time.

Hackett and Mick mutely agreed that things were clear.

– Down there you are likely to meet a personality who is from heaven, who is all-wise, speaks all languages and dialects and knows, or can know, everything. I have never had a companion on such a trip before, and I do hope events will not be complicated.

Mick had suddenly become very excited.

– Excuse the question, he blurted, but will this be John the Baptist again?

– No. At least I hope not. I can request but cannot command.

– Could it be . . . anybody? Hackett asked.

– Only the dead.

– Good heavens!

– Yet that is not wholly correct. Those who were never on earth could appear.

This little talk was eerie. It was as if a hangman were courteously conversing with his victim, on the scaffold high.

– Do you mean angels, Mr De Selby? Mick enquired.

– Deistic beings, he said gruffly. Here, stand still till I fix this.

He had picked up a breathing mask, with its straps and tank affair at the back.

– I'll go after you, Mick muttered, with Hackett at the rear.

In a surprisingly short time they were all fully dressed for a visit under the sea to the next world, or perhaps the former world. Through his goggles Mick could see Teague McGettigan studying an early Sunday paper, apparently at a rear racing page. He was at peace, with no interest whatever in supernatural doings. He was perhaps to be envied. Hackett was standing impassive, an Apollo space-man. De Selby was making final adjustments to his straps and with a gesture had led the way to the lower board.

Going head-down into cold water in the early morning is a shock to the most practised. But in Mick's case the fog of doubt and near-delusion in the head, added to by the very low hiss of his air supply, made it a brief but baffling experience. There was ample light as he followed De Selby's kicking heels and a marked watery disturbance behind told him that Hackett was not far away. If he was cursing, nobody heard.

Entry to the 'apartment' was efficient enough for beginners. If not adroit. De Selby readily found the opening and then, one by one, the others made their way upwards, half-clambering, half-swimming. They left the water quite palpably and Mick found himself crouching in an empty space on a rough floor strewn with rocks and some shells. Everything was dark and a distant sussurus must have been from the sea which had just been left. The company was under the water and presumably in an atmosphere that could be breathed, though only for a short time. *Time?* Yes, the word might be repeated.

De Selby beckoned Mick on with a tug at the arm, and he did the same for Hackett behind. Then they stopped. Mick crouched and finally squatted on a roundish rock; De Selby was to his left and the three had come to some sort of resting posture. Hackett gave Mick a nudge, though the latter did not know if it meant commiseration, encouragement or derision.

From his movements it was evident even in the gloom that De Selby was busy at some technical operation. Mick could not see what he was doing but no doubt he was detonating (or whatever is the word) a minuscule charge of D.M.P.

Though wet, he did not feel cold, but he was apprehensive, puzzled, curious. Hackett was near but quite still.

A faint light seemed to come, a remote glow. It gradually grew to define the dimension of the dim apartment, making it appear unexpectedly large and, strangely dry.

Then Mick saw a figure, a spectre, far away from him. It looked seated and slightly luminescent. Gradually it got rather clearer in definition but remained unutterably distant, and what he had taken for a very long chin in profile was almost certainly a beard. A gown of some dark material clothed the apparition. It is strange to say that the manifestation did not frighten him but he was flabbergasted when he heard De Selby's familiar tones almost booming out beside him.

— I must thank you for coming. I have two students with me.

The voice that came back was low, from far away but perfectly clear. The Dublin accent was unmistakable. The extraordinary utterance can here be distinguished only typographically.

— *Ah not at all man.*

— You're feeling well, as usual, I suppose?

— *Nothing to complain of, thank God. How are you feeling yourself, or how do you think you're feeling?*

— Tolerably, but age is creeping in.

— *Ha-ha. That makes me laugh.*

— Why?

— *Your sort of time is merely a confusing index of decomposition. Do you remember what you didn't know was your youth?*

— I do. But it's *your* youth I wanted to talk about. The nature of your life in youth compared with that of your hagiarchic senility must have been a thunderous contrast, the ascent to piety sudden and even distressing. Was it?

— *You are hinting at anoxic anoxæmia? Perhaps.*

— You admit you were a debauched and abandoned young man?

— *For a pagan I wasn't the worst. Besides, maybe it was the Irish in me.*

— The Irish in you?

— *Yes. My father's name was Patrick. And he was a proper gobshite.*

— Do you admit that the age or colour of women didn't matter to you where the transaction in question was coition?

— *I'm not admitting anything. Please remember my eyesight was very poor.*

— Were all your rutting ceremonials heterosexual?

— *Heterononsense! There is no evidence against me beyond*

34

what I wrote myself. Too vague. Be on your guard against that class of fooling. Nothing in black and white.
– My vocation is enquiry and action, not literature.
– *You're sadly inexperienced. You cannot conceive the age I lived in, its customs, or judge of that African sun.*
– The heat, hah? I've read a lot about the Eskimoes. The poor bastards are perished throughout their lives, covered with chilblains and icicles but when they catch a seal – ah, good luck to them! They make warm clothes out of the hide, perform gluttonly feats with the meat and then bring the oil home to the igloo where they light lamps and stoves. Then the fun begins. Nanook of the North is certainly partial to his nookie.
– *I reprobate concupiscence, whether fortuitous or contrived.*
– You do *now*, you post-gnostic! You must have a red face to recall your earlier nasty gymnastiness, considering you're now a Father of the Church.
– *Rubbish. I invented obscene feats out of bravado, lest I be thought innocent or cowardly. I walked the streets of Babylon with low companions, sweating from the fires of lust. When I was in Carthage I carried about with me a cauldron of unrealized debauchery. God in his majesty was tempting me. But Book Two of my Confessions is all shocking exaggeration. I lived within my rough time. And I kept the faith, unlike a lot more of my people in Algeria who are now Arab nincompoops and slaves of Islam.*
– Look at all the time you squandered in the maw of your sexual fantasies which otherwise could have been devoted to Scriptural studies. Lolling loathsome libertine!
– *I was weak at the time but I find your condescension offensive. You talk of the Fathers. How about that ante-Nicene thooleramawn, Origen of Alexandria? What did he do when he found that lusting after women distracted him from his sacred scrivenery? I'll tell you. He stood up, hurried out to the kitchen, grabbed a carving knife and – pwitch! –*

35

in one swipe deprived himself of his personality! Ah?
– Yes. Let us call it heroic impetuosity.
– *How could Origen be the Father of Anything and he with no knackers on him? Answer me that one.*
– We must assume that his spiritual testicles remained intact. Do you know him?
– *I can't say I ever met him in our place.*
– But, dammit is he there? Don't you know everything?
– *I do not. I can, but the first wisdom is sometimes not to know. I suppose I could ask the Polyarch.*
– Who on earth is the Polyarch?
– *He's not on earth, and again I don't know. I think he's Christ's Vicar in Heaven.*
– Are there any other strange denizens?
– *Far too many if you ask me. Look at that gobhawk they call Francis Xavier. Hobnobbing and womanizing in the slums of Paris with Calvin and Ignatius Loyola in warrens full of rats, vermin, sycophants, and syphilis. Xavier was a great travelling man, messing about in Ethiopia and Japan, consorting with Buddhist monkeys and planning to convert China single-handed. And Loyola? You talk about me but a lot of that chap's early saintliness was next to bedliness. He made himself the field-marshal of a holy army of mendicants but maybe merchandizers would be more like it. Didn't Pope Clement XIV suppress the Order for its addiction to commerce, and for political wire-pulling? Jesuits are the wiliest, cutest and most mendacious ruffians who ever lay in wait for simple Christians. The Inquisition was on the track of Ignatius. Did you know that? Pity they didn't get him. But one party who wouldn't hear of the Pope's Brief of Suppression was the Empress of Rooshia. Look at that now!*
– Interesting that your father's name was Patrick. Is he a saint?
– *That reminds me. You have a Professor Binchy in your university outfit in Dublin and that poor man has been writing and preaching since he was a boy that the story about*

36

Saint Patrick is all wrong and that there were really two
Saint Patricks. Binchy has his hash and parsley.
– Why?
– *Two Saint Patricks? We have* four *of the buggers in our
place and they'd make you sick with their shamrocks and
shenanigans and bullshit.*
– Who else? What about Saint Peter?
– *Oh he's safe and sound all right. A bit of a slob to tell you
the truth. He often encorpifies himself.*
– What was that?
– *Encorpifies himself. Takes on a body, as I've done now for
your convenience. How could the like of you make anything
out of an infinity of gases? Peter's just out to show off the
keys, bluster about and make himself a bloody nuisance. Oh
there have been a few complaints to the Polyarch about him.*
– Answer me this question. The Redeemer said 'Thou art
Peter and upon this rock I shall found my Church'. Is there
any justification for the jeer that He founded his Church
upon a pun, since *Petros* means 'rock'?
– *Not easy to say. The name Petros does not occur in classical, mythological or biblical Greek apart from your man the
apostle and his successor and later namesakes – except for a
freedman of Berenice (mother of Herod Agrippa) mentioned
in Josephus,* Jewish Antiquities 18, 6, 3, *in a passage relating
to the later years of Tiberius's reign, that is, the thirties* A.D.
Petro occurs as a Roman surname in Suetonius's Vespasiae
1, *and Petra as a woman's name in Tacitus,* Annals 11, 4.
– And you don't care a lot about him?
– *The lads in our place, when he barges around encorpified
and flashing the keys, can't resist taking a rise out of him and
pursue him with the cackles of a rooster, cock-adoodle-doo.*
– I see. Who else? Is Judas with you?
– *That's another conundrum for the Polyarch. Peter
stopped me one time and tried to feed me a cock-and-bull
story about Judas coming to the Gate. You get my joke?
Cock-and-bull story?*

37

– Very funny. Is your mother Monica there?

– *Wait now! Don't try and get a dig at me that way. Don't blame me. She was here before me.*

– To lower the temperature of your steaming stewpot of lust and depravity, you married or took as concubine a decent poor young African girl, and the little boy you had by her you named Adeodatus. But even yet nobody knows your wife's name.

– *That secret is safe with me still.*

– Why should you give such a name to your son while you were yourself still a debauched pagan, not even baptized?

– *Put that day's work down to the mammy – Monica.*

– Later, you put your little wife away and she shambled off to the wilderness, probably back into slavery, but swearing to remain faithful to you forever. Does the shame of that come back to you?

– *Never mind what comes back to me, I done what the mammy said, and everybody – you too – has to do what the mammy says.*

– And straightaway, as you relate in Book Six of your Confessions, you took another wife, simultaneously committing bigamy and adultery. And you kicked her out after your *Tolle Lege* conjuring tricks in the garden when you ate a handful of stolen pears. Eve herself wasn't accused in respect of more than one apple. In all this disgraceful behaviour do we see Monica at work again?

– *Certainly. God also.*

– Does Monica know that you're being so unprecedentedly candid with me?

– Know? *She's probably here unencorpified.*

– You betrayed and destroyed two decent women, implicated God in giving a jeering name to a bastard, and you blame all this outrage on your mother. Would it be seemly to call you callous humbug?

– *It would not. Call me a holy humbug.*

– Who else is in your kingdom? Is Judas?

— Paul is in our place, often encorpified and always attended by his physician Luke, putting poultices on his patient's sore neck. When Paul shows too much consate in himself, the great blatherskite with his epistles in bad Greek, the chronic two-timer, I sometimes roar after him 'You're not on the road to Damascus now!' Puts him in his place. All the same that Tolle Lege incident was no conjuring trick. It was a miracle. The first book I picked up was by Paul and the lines that struck my eyes were these: 'Not in rioting or drunkenness, nor in chambering or wantonness, nor in strife or envying: but put ye on the Lord Jesus Christ and make not provision for the flesh in the lust thereof.' But do you know, I think the greatest dog's breakfast of the lot is St Vianney.

— I never heard of him.

— 'Course you have. Jean-Baptiste. You'd know him better as the curé of Ars.

— Oh yes. A French holy man.

— A holy fright, you mean. Takes a notion when he's young to be a priest, as ignorant as the back of a cab, couldn't make head nor tail of Latin or sums, dodges the column when Napoleon is looking for French lads to be slaughtered in Rooshia, and at the heel of the hunt spends sixteen to eighteen hours a day in the confessional — hearing, not telling — and takes to performing miracles, getting money from nowhere and taking on hand to tell the future. Don't be talking. A diabolical wizard of a man.

— Your household abounds in oddities.

— He performs his miracles still in our place. Gives life to bogus corpses and thinks nothing of raising from the dead a dummy mummy.

— I repeat a question I've already asked: is Judas a member of your household?

— I don't think the Polyarch would like me to say much about Judas.

— He particularly interests me. The Gospel extols love and

justice. Peter denied his Master out of pride, vanity and perhaps fear. Judas did something similar but from a comprehensible motive. But Peter's home and dried. Is Judas?

– *Judas, being dead, is eternal.*

– But where is he?

– *The dead do not have whereness. They have condition.*

– Did Judas earn paradise?

– *Pulchritudo tam antiqua et tam nova sero amavit.*

– You are shifty and you prevaricate. Say yes or no to this question: did you suffer from hæmorrhoids?

– *Yes. That is one reason that I encorpify myself with reluctance.*

– Did Judas have any physical affliction?

– *You have not read my works. I did not build the City of God. At most I have been an humble urban district councillor, never the Town Clerk. Whether Judas is dead in the Lord is a question notice of which would require to be given to the Polyarch.*

– De Quincey held that Judas enacted his betrayal to provoke his Master into proclaiming his divinity by deed. What do you think of that?

– *De Quincey also consumed narcotics.*

– Nearly everything you have taught or written lacks the precision of Descartes.

– *Descartes was a recitalist, or formulist, of what he took, often mistakenly, to be true knowledge. He himself established nothing new, nor even a system of pursuing knowledge that was novel. You are fond of quoting his* Cogito Ergo Sum. *Read my works. He stole that. See my dialogue with Evodius in* De Libero Arbitrio, *or the Question of Free Choice. Descartes spent far too much time in bed subject to the persistent hallucination that he was thinking. You are not free from a similar disorder.*

– I have read all the philosophy of the Fathers, before and after Nicaea: Chrysostom, Ambrose, Athanasius.

– *If you have read Athanasius you have not understood*

him. The result of your studies might be termed a corpus of patristic paddeology.

– Thank you.

– *You are welcome.*

– The prime things – existence, time, the godhead, death, paradise and the satanic pit, these are abstractions. Your pronouncements on them are meaningless, and within itself the meaninglessness does not cohere.

– *Discourse must be in words, and it is possible to give a name to that which is not understood nor cognoscible by human reason. It is our duty to strive towards God by thought and word. But it is our final duty to believe, to have and to nourish faith.*

– I perceive some of your pronouncements to be heretical and evil. Of sin, you said it was necessary for the perfection of the universe and to make good shine all the more brightly in contrast. You said God is not the cause of our doing evil but that free will is the cause. From God's omniscience and foreknowledge He knows that men will sin. How then could free will exist?

– *God has not foreknowledge. He is, and has knowledge.*

– Man's acts are all subject to predestination and he cannot therefore have free will. God created Judas. Saw to it that he was reared, educated, and should prosper in trade. He also ordained that Judas should betray His Divine Son. How then could Judas have guilt?

– *God, in knowing the outcome of free will, did not thereby attenuate or extirpate free will.*

– That light-and-shade gentleman you once admired so much, Mani, held that Cain and Abel were not the sons of Adam and Eve but the sons of Eve and Satan. However that may be, the sin in the garden of Eden was committed in an unimaginably remote age, eons of centuries ago, according to the mundane system of computing time. According to the same system the doctrine of the Incarnation and the Re- demption is now not even two thousand years old. Are all the millions and millions of uncountable people born between the Creation and the Redemption to be accounted lost, dying in original sin though themselves personally guiltless, and to be considered condemned to hell?

– If you would know God, you must know time. God is time. God is the substance of eternity. God is not distinct from what we regard as years. God has no past, no future, no presence in the sense of man's fugitive tenure. The interval you mention between the Creation and the Redemption was ineffably unexistent.

– That is the sort of disputation that I dub 'flannel' but granted that the soul of man is immortal, the geometry of a soul must be circular and, like God, it cannot have had a beginning. Do you agree with that?

– In piety it could thus be argued.

– Then our souls existed before joining our bodies?

– That could be said.

– Well, where were they?

– None but the Polyarch would say that.

– Are we to assume there is in existence somewhere a boundless reservoir of souls not yet encorpified?

– Time does not enter into an act of divine creation. God can create something which has the quality of having always existed.

– Is there any point in my questioning you on your one-time devotion to the works of Plotinus and Porphyry?

– No. But far preferable to the Manichæan dualism of light and darkness, good and evil, was Plotinus's dualism of mind and matter. In his doctrine of emanation Plotinus was only slightly misled. Plotinus was a good man.

– About 372, when you were eighteen, you adopted Manichæanism and did not discard the strange creed until ten years later. What do you think now that jumble of Babylonian cosmology, Buddhism and ghostly theories about light and darkness, the Elect and the Hearers, the commands to abstain from fleshmeat, manual labour and intercourse with women? Or Mani's own claim that he was himself the Paraclete?

— *Why ask me now when you can read the treatise against this heresy which I wrote in 394? So far as Mani himself is concerned, my attitude maybe be likened to that of the King of Persia in 376. He had Mani skinned alive and then crucified.*

— We must be going very soon.

— *Yes. Your air is nearly gone.*

— There is one more question on a matter that has always baffled me and on which nothing written about you by yourself or others gives any illumination. *Are you a Nigger?*

— *I am a Roman.*

— I suspect your Roman name is an affectation or a disguise. You are of Berber stock, born in Numidia. Those people were non-white. You are far more aligned with Carthage than Rome, and there are Punic corruptions even in your Latin.

— *Civis Romanus sum.*

— The people of your homeland today are called Arabs. Arabs are not white.

— *Berbers were blond white people, with lovely blue eyes.*

— All true Africans, notwithstanding the racial stew in that continent, are to some extent niggers. They are descendants of Noah's son Ham.

— *You must not overlook the African sun. I was a man that was very easily sunburnt.*

— What does it feel like to be in heaven for all eternity?

— *For all eternity? Do you then think there are fractional or temporary eternities?*

— If I ask it, will you appear to me here tomorrow?

— *I have no tomorrow. I am. I have only nowness.*

— Then we shall wait. Thanks and goodbye.

— *Goodbye. Mind the rocks. Go with God.*

With clambering, Hackett in the lead, they soon found the water and made their way back to this world.

43

5

The morning was still there, bland as they had left it. Teague McGettigan was slumped in charge of his pipe and newspaper and gave them only a glance when, having discarded their masks, they proceeded without thought to brisk towelling.

– Well, De Selby called to Mick, what did you think of that?

Mentally, Mick felt numb, confused; and almost surprised by ordinary day.

– That was ... an astonishing apparition, he stammered. And I heard every word. A very shrewd and argumentative man whoever he was.

De Selby froze in his half-naked stance, his mouth falling a bit open in dismay.

– Great crucified Lord, he cried, don't tell me you didn't recognize Augustine?

Mick stared back, still benumbed.

– I thought it was Santa Claus, Hackett remarked. Yet his voice lacked the usual intonation of jeer.

– I suppose, De Selby mused, beginning to dress, that I do you two some injustice. I should have warned you. A first encounter with a man from heaven can be unnerving.

– Several of the references were familiar enough, Mick said, but I couldn't quite pinpoint the personality. My goodness, the Bishop of Hippo!

– Yes. When you think of it, he did not part with much information.

– If I may say so, Hackett interposed, he didn't seem too happy in heaven. Where was the glorious resurrection we've all been promised? That character underground wouldn't get a job handing out toys in a store at Christmas. He seemed depressed.

– I must say that the antics of his companions seemed

strange, Mick agreed. I mean, according to his account of them.

De Selby stopped reflectively combing his sparse hair.

– One must reserve judgement on all such manifestations, he said. I am proceeding all the time on a theory. We should remember that that might not have been the genuine Augustine at all.

– But who, then?

The wise master stared out to sea.

– It could be even Beelzebub himself, he murmured softly.

Hackett sat down abruptly, working at his tie.

– Have any of you gentlemen got a match? Teague McGettigan asked, painfully standing up. Hackett handed him a box.

– The way I see it, Teague continued, there will come an almighty clump of rain and wind out of Wickla about twelve o'clock. Them mountains down there has us all destroyed.

– I'm not afraid of a shower, Hackett remarked coldly. At least you know what it is. There are worse things.

– Peaks of rock prod up into the clouds like fingers, Teague explained, until the clouds is bursted and the wind carries the wather down here on top of us. Poor buggers on a walking tour around Shankill would get soaked, hang-sangwiches in sodden flitters and maybe not the price of a pint between them to take shelter in Byrnes.

Their dressing, by reason of their rough rig, was finished. De Selby and Hackett were smoking, and the time was half nine. Then De Selby energetically rubbed his hands.

– Gentlemen, he said with some briskness, I presume that like me you have had no breakfast before this early swim. May I therefore invite you to have breakfast with me at Lawnmower. Mr McGettigan can drive us up to the gate.

– I'm afraid I can't go, Hackett said.

– Well, it's not that my horse Jimmy couldn't pull you up, Teague said, spitting.

– Come now, De Selby said, we all need inner fortification

after an arduous morning. I have peerless Limerick rashers and there will be no shortage of that apéritif.

Whether or not Hackett had another engagement Mick did not know but he immediately shared his instinct to get away, if only, indeed, to think, or try not to think. De Selby had not been deficient in the least in manners or honourable conduct but his continuing company seemed to confer uneasiness – perhaps vague, unformed fear.

– Mr De Selby, Mick said warmly, it is indeed kind of you to invite Hackett and me up for a meal but it happens that I did in fact have breakfast. I think we'd better part here.

– We'll meet soon again, Hackett remarked, to talk over this morning's goings-on.

De Selby shrugged and beckoned McGettigan to help him with his gear.

– As you will, gentlemen, he said politely enough. I certainly could do with a bite and perhaps I will have the pleasure of Teague's company. I thought the weather, the elements, all the forces of the heavens made a breakfast-tide lecture seemly.

– Good luck to your honour but there's nourishment in that bottle you have, Teague said brightly, taking away his pipe to say it loudly.

They separated like that and Hackett and Mick went on their brief stroll into Dalkey, Mick wheeling the bicycle with some distaste.

– Have you somewhere to go? he asked.

– No I haven't. What did you make of that performance?

– I don't know what to say. You heard the conversation, and I presume both of us heard the same thing.

– Do you believe . . . it all happened?

– I suppose I have to.

– I need a drink.

They fell silent. Thinking about the séance (if that ill-used word will serve) was futile though disturbing and yet it was impossible to shut such thoughts out of the head. Somehow

Mick saw little benefit in any discussion with Hackett. Hackett's mind was twisted in a knot identical with his own. They were as two tramps who had met in a trackless desert, each hopelessly asking the other the way.

— Well, Hackett said moodily at last, I haven't thrown overboard my suspicions of yesterday about drugs, and even hypnotism I wouldn't quite discount. But we have no means of checking whether or not all that stuff this morning was hallucination.

— Couldn't we ask somebody? Get advice?

— Who? For a start, who would believe a word of the story?

— That's true.

— Incidentally, those underwater breathing masks were genuine. I've worn gadgets like that before but they weren't as smart as De Selby's.

— How do we know there wasn't a mixture of some brain-curdling gas in the air-tank?

— That's true by God,

— I quite forgot I was wearing the thing.

They had paused undecided at a corner in the lonely little town. Mick said that he thought he'd better go home and get some breakfast. Hackett thought it was too early to think of food. Well Mick had to get rid of his damned bike. Couldn't he leave it at the comic little police station in charge of Sergeant Fottrell? But what was the point of that? Wouldn't he have the labour of collecting it another time? Hackett said that there had been no necessity to have used it at all in the first place, as there was such a thing as an early tram to accommodate eccentric people. Mick said no, not on Sunday, not from Booterstown.

— I know Mrs L would let me in, Hackett observed pettishly, except I know the big sow is still in bed snoring.

— Yes, it's been a funny morning, Mick replied sympathetically. Here you are, frustrated from joining the company of a widow who keeps a boozer, yet it is not half an hour since you parted company with Saint Augustine.

47

– Yes.

Hackett laughed bitterly. Mick had in fact business of his own later in the day, he remembered, as on nearly every Sunday. At three-thirty he would meet Mary at Ballsbridge and very likely they would go off to loaf amorously and chatter in Herbert Park. The arrangement was threatening to take on the tedium of routine things. When eventually they were married, if they were at all, wouldn't the sameness of life be worse?

– I'm going to rest my mind, he announced, and rest it in Herbert Park later today, avec ma femme, ma bonne amie.

– My own Asterisk lady abstains on Sundays, Hackett said listlessly, lighting a cigarette.

But suddenly he came to life.

– Consternation was caused this morning, he cried, by the setting off of a small charge of D.M.P. Here comes the D.M.P. in person!

True enough. Wheeling a bicycle, Sergeant Fottrell was coming towards them from a side road. His approach was slow and grave. Here one beheld the majesty of the law – inevitable, procedural, sure.

It is not easy to outline his personal portrait. He was tall, lean, melancholy, clean-shaven, red in the face and of indeterminate age. Nobody, it was said, had ever seen him in uniform, yet he was far from being a plain-clothes man; his constabulary was unmistakable. Summer and winter he wore a light tweed overcoat of a brown colour; a trace of collar and tie could be discerned about the neck but in his nether person the trousers were clearly of police blue, and the large boots also surely of police issue. Dr Crewett claimed to have seen the sergeant once with his overcoat off when assisting with a broken-down car and no inner jacket of any kind was disclosed, only shirt. The sergeant was friendly, so to speak, to his friends. He drank whiskey freely when the opportunity offered but it did not seem to affect him at all. Hackett held that this was because the sergeant's normal

48

sober manner was identical with the intoxicated manner of other people. But what the sergeant believed, what he said and how he said it was known throughout all south County Dublin.

Now he had stopped and saluted at his cloth cap.

— That's the great morning, lads, he said, gratuitously.

There was agreement that it was. The sergeant seemed to be maturing the air and the early street.

— I see you have been to the water, he remarked genially, for far-from-simple cavortings in the brine?

— Sergeant, Hackett said, you have no idea how far from simple.

— I recede portentously from the sea, the sergeant beamed, except for a fastidious little wade for the good of my spawgs. For the truth is that I'm destroyed with the corns. Our work is walking work if you understand my portent.

— True enough, Sergeant, Mick agreed, I have often seen you with that bicycle but never up on it.

— It is emergency machinery for feats of captaincy. But there are dangers of a mental nature inherent in the bicycle and that story I will relate to you coherently upon another day.

— Yes.

Hackett was meditating on something.

— Funny thing, he said, I left a little bottle behind me in the Colza last night by accident. Perigastric thiosulphate, you know. My damned stomach is full of ructions and eructations.

— Well by damn, the sergeant sighed sympathetically, that is an infertile bitching. I cry for any creature, man or woman, who is troublous in the stomach enpitments. Mrs Laverty would be in her bed now or mayhap awash in her private bath internally.

— Brandy is good for a sick stomach, Mick ventured with studied tactlessness.

— Brandy? Baugh! Hackett grimaced.

— Not brandy but Brannigan, the sergeant cried, striking his crossbar. Brannigan the chemist, and he's an early-Mass man. He would now be shovelling gleefully at his stirabout, and supinely dietetic. Come down along here now.

Glumly Mick followed Hackett's downcast back as the sergeant led the way down the street to a corner shop and smartly knocked on the residential door. The small meek Mr Brannigan had scarcely opened it when they were all crowded in the hallway. Mick felt annoyed at this improvised and silly tactic. What would passers-by think of two bicycles outside at such an hour, with the sergeant's the most recognizable in the whole country? Hackett might be forced to swallow a dose of salts rather than disavow his lie about digestion trouble, and good enough for him.

— I have a man here, Mr Brannigan, avic, the sergeant announced cheerfully, that has a raging confusion in his craw, a stainless citizen and a martyr. Let us make our way sedulously to the shop.

Mr Brannigan with vague noises had produced keys and opened a door in the narrow hall; then they were all in the shop, with its gaudy goods and showcases. Under the high ceiling Mr Brannigan looked tiny (or perhaps his nearness to the sergeant was the real reason), the face quite round, round glasses in it and an air of being pleased.

— Which of the gentlemen, Sergeant, he asked quietly, is out of humour with himself?

The sergeant clapped a hand officially on Hackett's shoulder.

— Mr Hackett is the patient inexorably, he said.

— Ah. Where is the seat of the trouble, Mr Hackett?

The patient made a clutching motion at his stomach.

— Here, he muttered, where nearly everybody's damn trouble lies.

— Ah-ha. Have you been taking anything in particular for it?

— I have. But I can't tell you what. Something from a prescription I haven't got on me.

— Well well now. I would recommend a mix of acetic an-
hydride with carbonic acid. In solution. Excellent stuff in the
right proportions. I won't be a minute getting it.

— No, no, Hackett said in genuine remonstrance. I daren't
take drugs I'm not used to. Very nice of you and the Sergeant, Mr Brannigan, but I can wait.

— But we've any amount of proprietary things here, Mr
Hackett. Even temporary relief, you know . . .

But the sergeant had been examining a large bottle he had
taken down from a low shelf by the counter.

— By the pipers, he cried happily, here is the elixir of youth
innocuously in its mundane perfection !

He handed the bottle to Hackett and reached up for
another which he put in Mick's hand. The label was,

HURLEY'S TONIC WINE

A glass three times a day or as required assures lasting benefit to
the kidneys, stomach and nervous system. As recommended by
doctors, nurses and geriatric institutions.

— Mind you, that's not a bad sedative for the inner man, Mr
Brannigan said seriously. Many ladies in the town are very
partial to it.

— Sir Thomas O'Brannigan, the sergeant intoned grandly, I
will buy a bottle of it myself – put it down to me – and when
you have emplaced delicate stem glasses we will all have a
sup of it superbly, for the dear knows how sick we could all
be in the heel of the day.

Mr Brannigan smiled and nodded. Hackett hastily examined their faces in the uncertain light.

— I suppose it would pull us together a bit, he conceded. I'll
have a bottle too.

That Sunday morning had been surely one of mani-
coloured travail. After acerb disputation between De Selby
and Saint Augustine, here they were for at least an hour in
that closed pharmacy drinking Hurley's Tonic Wine and
listening to Sergeant Fottrell's *pensées* on happiness, health,

the wonders of foreign travel, law and order, and bicycles. The tonic was, as one suspected it would be, a cheap red wine heavily fortified. Its social purpose was clear enough. It enabled prim ladies, who would be shocked at the idea of entering a public house, to drink liquor that was by no means feeble, in the defensible interest of promoting health.

Mick had also bought a bottle and they were in the midst of a fourth bottle which Mr Brannigan had gallantly put up 'on the house' when Mick felt that sheer shame required that the little party should end. Hackett agreed that he felt much better but not so Mick; even genuine wine does not help much, and he felt a little bit queasy. The sergeant was quite unmoved, and undeterred in loquacity. When they were back in the street Mick turned to him.

– Sergeant, the day is getting older and more people are now about. Would you mind if I left this bike in your station till tomorrow? I think for me a tram home would be the business.

– Benignly certain, he replied, courteously. Tell Policeman Pluck that I ordained the custody unceremoniously.

He then departed about his public business with many blessings commending his friends to God.

– Do you know, Hackett mentioned as they moved off, all that Augustinian chat is gradually bringing half-forgotten things bubbling up in my head. Didn't he have a ferocious go at Pelagius?

– The heretic? Yes.

– What do you mean heretic?

– That's what he was. Some synod condemned and ex-communicated him.

– I thought only the Pope could pronounce on heresy.

– No. He appealed to the Pope without result.

– I see. Other bad eggs were the Manichees and the Donat-ists. I know that. I don't mind about them at all. But if my memory isn't all bunched, I believe Pelagius was a grand man and a sound theologian.

– You don't know much on the subject. Don't pretend.

– He believed Adam's lapse (and personally I wouldn't take the slightest notice of such fooling) harmed only himself. The guilt was his alone and this yarn about everybody being born in original sin is all bloody bull.

– Oh, as you will.

– Who, believing in God, could also believe that the whole human race was prostrate in ruin before Christ came, the day before yesterday?

– Augustine, for one, I think.

– New-born infants are innocent and if they die before baptism, they have a right to heaven. Baptism is only a rite, a sort of myth.

– According to De Selby, John the Baptist was no myth. He met the man. He probably regards him as a personal friend.

– Are *you* baptized?

– I suppose so.

– Suppose so? Is a hazy opinion enough if your soul depends on it?

– For heaven's sake shut up. Haven't we had enough for today and yesterday?

– An awkward question, what?

At this rate I'll probably meet Martin Luther on top of the tram.

Hackett contemptuously lit a cigarette and stopped.

– I'll leave you here, go for a walk, get a paper, sit down and read a lot of boring muck, and wait for a chance to slip into the Colza. But remember this: *I'm a Pelagian.*

Policeman Pluck was young, raw-boned, mottled of complexion and wore an expression of friendly stupidity. He had a bicycle upside-down on the floor of the day-room attending to a hernia at the front rim, grating white powder on to a protruding intestine. His salute for Mick was an inane smile in which his scrupulously correct uniform seemed to concur,

53

though all visible teeth seemed to be bad and discoloured.

– Morning, Mr Pluck. I met the sergeant and he told me I could leave this other machine here for a day or two. I'll get a tram.

– Well he did, did he? grinned Policeman Pluck. Ah, the dacent lovable man!

– Is that all right?

– You are welcome sir, and lave it be the wall there. But the sergeant's tune will change when he comes up with that cabman Teague.

– What has Teague done?

Policeman Pluck blanched slightly at the recollection of horror.

– Yesterday he met a missionary father, a Redempiorist, at the station and druv him up to the parochial house. Well, Teague and his jinnet wasn't five minits in the P.P.'s holy grounds but before they left it they had the whole place in a pukey mess of a welter of dung.

– Ah, unfortunate, that.

– Enough to dress two drills of new spring spuds.

– Still, Teague was hardly to blame.

– Do you expect the sergeant to have the jinnet in the dock for sacrilege? Or for a sin against the Holy Ghost? I'll tell you wan thing boy.

– What's that?

– You'll have a scarifying mission, an iron mission, there will be rosaries on the bended knees for further orders, starting tomorra. There'll be hell to pay. But thank God it's the weemen's week first.

– Thank God, Mr Pluck, Mick called back at the door, I'm not even a parishioner.

Why should he take account of hellfire sermons anyway? Had he not been, in a kind of a way, in heaven?

6

Mary was not a simple girl, not an easy subject to write about nor Mick the one to write. He thought women in general were hopeless as a theme for discussion or discourse, and surely for one man the one special – *la femme particulière,* if that sharpens the meaning – must look dim, meaningless and empty to others if he should talk genuinely about her or think aloud. The mutual compulsion is a mystery, not just a foible or biogenesis, and this sort of mystery, even if comprehensible to the two concerned, is at least absolutely private.

Mary was no sweetie-pie nor was she pretty but (to Mick's eyes) she was good-looking and dignified. Brown-eyed, her personality was russet and usually she was quiet and recollected. He was, he thought, very fond of her and did not by any means regard her as merely a member of her sex, or anything so commonplace and trivial. She was a true obsession with him (he suspected) and kept coming into his head on all sorts of irrelevant occasions without, so to speak, knocking. Hackett's relations with the peculiar girl he mixed around with seemed perfunctory, like having a taste for marmalade at breakfast or meditatively paring· fingernails in public-house silences.

Mick was absolutely sure in mind about few things but he thought he could sincerely say that Mary was an unusual girl. She was educated, with a year in France, and understood music. She had wit, could be lively, and it took little to induce for a while gaiety of word and mood. Her people, whom he did not know, had money. She was tasteful and fastidious in dress . . . and why not? She worked in what was called a fashion house, with a top job which Mick knew paid well and involved consorting only with people of standing. Her job was one thing they had never talked about. That her earnings were a secret was something he was deeply thankful for because he knew that they could scarcely be less than his own. A disclosure, even accidental, would be his humiliation though he knew all this situation was very silly. Yet work at the fol-the-lols of couture did nothing to impair Mary's maturity of mind. She read a lot, talked politics often and once even mentioned her half-intention of writing a book. Mick did not ask on what subject, for somehow he found the idea distasteful. Without swallowing whole all the warnings one could readily hear and read about the spiritual dangers of intellectual arrogance and literary freebooting, there *was* menace in the overpoise that high education and a rich way of living could confer on a young girl. Unknowingly, she could exceed her own strength. Did she find his own company a stabilizing pull? Mick had to doubt that, for the truth was that he was not too steady himself. Confession once a month was all very well but he was drinking too much. He would give up drink. Also, he would make Mary more of his own quiet kind, and down to earth.

Yet what was the real position about him and her? Uncertain. He was going to marry her, that was intended. And that was one other subject never mentioned outright in all the long three years of their togetherness. His rotten job, poor pay and worse prospects were always there, physical and repulsive manifestations, like erysipelas. But what other course was open to him? To her, even? In some unthinkable extremity he might perhaps turn to a sad celibacy, yet if somebody else were to come and carry her away, he was sure he would take leave of his senses. He would do some frightful thing, quite stupid but unavoidable.

They were in Herbert Park.

Lolling on a sloping bank of short grass near the lake where ducks and toy boats were moving in a mild uproar of children, their talk had been desultory. He was not anxious to present for inspection his new spiritual status – yet, he asked himself, was she not entitled to know?

– I didn't see you at Mass this morning, she remarked. Was this an opening for him? She was smoking but there was nothing rank, in the Hackett sense, about the fumes. She was a lady, and entitled to a cigarette. Sophistication, call it.

– No. I went off very early for a swim at Dalkey.

– With Hackett?

– Yes.

– Well that's something new. Swimming is all right but getting up at dawn for it, surely that's a rather British attitude? But Hackett up early on Sunday is something startling.

– Stranger things happen.

– How does he like the water when he's absolutely sober?

– We were meeting another man at the Vico. We wanted to be on our own to do some underwater exploration.

– Who was the other man – anybody I know?

– Hardly. We'd only met him ourselves the day before.

– Marine biology with some Trinity College chap – would that be it?

– No, no, a very queer hawk to tell you the truth, Mary, though we did also meet a lad from Trinity.

– Well, well. That makes four.

– Now don't confuse things. The Trinity poet fellow wasn't with us at all this morning.

– But this queer fellow. How queer was he?

Mick gazed about the gentle trees, the shrubs, the flowers, the motley people with prams and noise. It was all normal, and even attractive. De Selby and his associates was another matter.

– I don't mean queer in any bad sense. He was a strange man. He had unusual notions about the world, the universe, time . . . a physicist, really.

– Yes?

– His ideas quite transcended this earth – this damn earth we're lying on now.

– Is that so? That Dalkey is a place I'll have to find out more

57

about. But about transcending this earth . . . the simplest priest does that every Sunday.

– Not quite in De Selby's way. That's his name – De Selby.

– De Selby? Sounds foreign. Probably a spy.

– Oh De Selby's no foreigner. Not a bit of him. If the way he talks is any sign he's a native of our beloved Ireland. And he doesn't like Ireland, or like anywhere else in this world.

– Don't tell me he's another angry patriot?

– Certainly not.

– What exactly are you driving at, Mick?

– It's hard to convey it, my sweet dote. Hard to believe it, too.

She sat up and looked at him as he sprawled there, his hand shading his face. Her curiosity was awakened but that was not what Mick wanted; not yet, anyhow. A proper talk might help a lot when his own mind was clearer and possibly his experience wider.

– What's going on, Mick? Tell me. Tell me your damned story if you have one.

He sat up to show at least that this wasn't fooling. Here was more of the messing in which he was so expert in accidentally involving himself.

– Mary, let me put this in a few separate sentences. They all tot up to a pretty strange state of affairs. It could even mean some danger.

– Well, *what*? Her voice was sharp.

– This man De Selby keeps unusual company when he's on his own, he said in a low, even voice that seemed to belie the message. One of his butties is Saint John the Baptist.

– Mick! God forgive you!

– I'm serious.

– What sort of talk is that? This is Sunday, not that that makes any difference.

– He's also met many other holy characters such as Tertullian, I think. And maybe Athanasius.

She was tense and frowning now.

58

– And don't leave out Hackett. You told me already Hackett was there.

He looked her steadily in her brown eyes.

– Quite true. And with him both of us met Saint Augustine.

There was a small silence here. Even the noise around about seemed muted. Mary lit a cigarette.

– Mick, she asked seriously, what's the purpose of all this bosh? Am I supposed to laugh?

– No indeed.

– Where did you meet Saint Augustine?

– Under the sea at Vico.

– *Under the sea?*

– Yes. The three of us.

– And what happened?

– There was a long and complicated talk between De Selby and Saint Augustine.

– How could people talk under the sea, apart from the fact that one of them has been dead for centuries?

– We were in a cave.

– This is absolute lunacy, Mick. You know that.

– Hackett and I couldn't do any talking but we were there, we could listen, and did.

Another silence. Absolute lunacy is what his talk sounded to Mick himself, but what choice had he if this matter was to be dragged up at all? Suddenly he felt glad Hackett had been there, otherwise he might join Mary in her inference that he had been the victim of delusions. And another thing, both of them had been dead sober.

– Was a feed of whiskey the foundation of this rigmarole?

– We had no drink whatsoever, any of us. And I'll tell you another thing about De Selby . . .

– Not that he had two heads?

– No. He is going to destroy the world.

– Good Lord! How?

– He claims he has the means. I don't pretend to understand it exactly, and can't explain it. It's a very abstruse, technical

59

matter. He has invented a sort of miraculous substance. De Selby can pollute and destroy the whole atmosphere, the air we breathe.

That account of their chat is not accurate, but it was substantially the way the queer experience was mentioned. And they did not stop there. Mary went on asking other questions, and expressing incredulity or mild ridicule. His attitude was a quiet one, polite, obdurate. He hinted a little at his personal blamelessness, his innocence, even his simplicity. The events had not been of his contriving. But all the same he took care to make it plain that he was not apologizing. He was himself and he had his little rights.

In the end Mary seemed to accept, not what he had so baldly related but the fact that something very unusual had really happened and, though evidently he was confused, he was not telling outlandish lies. That was something; a mysterious something, but something.

After a time they got up and strolled out towards Lansdowne Road. Of course the wide streets they walked were unnecessarily common, the people ordinary if not colourless, and for himself he was depressed. Why not? Mary was silent when not talking superficially.

It was near six when they stopped at a tree.

Mary said that she had two tickets for a certain musical event that night. Her tone was indolent. She did not feel very like going. Did he? He said no.

— This night please God I'll go to bed early, Mary. And sleep long and deeply without dreams.

— You're tired?

— Between this world and the next I'm worn out. But it's probably this dead heat.

— Yes, and the complications about De Selby. I'll think over what you told me and try to be serious. I have a sort of an idea. I'll tell you about it when I'm sure. We must have a talk together with Hackett. Give me a ring, as usual. And . . . listen, Mick.

– Yes, Mary?

– Have a few bottles of stout for your supper if you have any at home.

– Well . . . thanks for the suggestion? Yes, Mary.

Believe it or not, light or no light, they kissed as privately as possible under that tree.

And homeward bound, he dallied for a time at Crowe's. The evening congregation there was cheerful, the malt benevolent and bronze. Mary was a superb lady. Soon he felt more bright-minded. And he reaffirmed his vow to cut his whiskey-drinking right out. If it had to be something for the immediate future, there was nothing wrong with stout.

7

Surprisingly, what followed for Mick was a rest – short enough, only eight or nine days, but his mixed-up mind simmered down a good bit when the De Selby encounters were reconsidered in the quiet of a more rested head. Nothing whatever had happened, he reminded himself, but talk. True, there seemed to have been a breach of the natural order in that apparition of Augustine in the grotesque chamber under the wave but several explanations might be forthcoming, including that of a temporary psychic malaise, a phantasm such as would arise from taking mescalin or morphine. Hackett's suspicion that De Selby had administered a very slow-acting drug to them was by no means out of the question, though he regretted that instead of that ridiculous wine-bibbing session in the chemist's shop, the two of them had not instantly sat down and compared their experience in detail and verified that their recollections of the

De Selby–Augustine duologue were identical. Then Hackett was, of course, unreliable and impetuous while Mick personally had no scientific training in evaluating a strange occurrence in retrospect, though he would now know better how to receive any development it might be God's will to permit. Meanwhile he was in no hurry to revisit Dalkey, though his bicycle still rested there.

The telephone rang in the room he shared with three others in Dublin Castle, and he was beckoned to the instrument. That would be Mary. They had a bargain that such calls should be brief, for his own lack of privacy was total. It is hard to say why he hated others to hear his meaningless responses.

– I'm off to London tomorrow in the interest of furthering the holy cause of my firm, she said.

– For how long?

– About a week.

What she said next startled him a bit. She had had a talk with her mother, but no names mentioned; she had merely said that somebody she knew was troubled and perplexed, and she wondered what could be done. The mother had very strongly advised that this person should go and see Father Cobble at Milltown Park. He was a most kind and understanding man, and ever willing to counsel the wanderer.

– He's one of the Jesuit Fathers there, of course, Mary added. But do nothing till I get back. I may give Father Cobble a ring this evening to see how he's fixed. Meantime, keep away from that hotel in Dalkey. And Mick, mind yourself.

Well damn it, he thought – was this to be a development, an unexpected divagation, a new horizon? Back to his mind came Augustine's slighting references to St Ignatius and his Order. What irony was here, he timidly consulting a Jesuit about De Selby!

He chuckled to himself (a good sign, perhaps) as he returned to his arid papers. Time would tell.

62

But four days later the telephone rang again. Who could this be? He grunted acquiescence when a deep male voice mentioned his full name.

– Ah! My name is Cobble, Father George Cobble. A dear friend has mentioned your name to me. I rang to say that I would be most happy to see you at any time.

– That is very good of you but—

– Not at all, my dear boy. When any little shadow falls on one, as it may on any of us, that little shadow is better shared.

– Oh, I understand.

– When the little shadow is spread over a wider surface, it grows less opaque, and with God's grace it might disappear completely.

– Father, I had arranged to go away for about a week. A little holiday break, if you understand me.

– Well now. That is good and cheerful news. I believe you live in Dalkey.

– No, no. Booterstown.

– Ah yes. I see. You will be back tomorrow week, I am sure. That will be the first day of September. Would you have a cup of tea with me, say at six that evening, at the Royal Marine, Dunleary?

– That is most kind of you. You see, it is another person I wanted to talk about.

– Excellent. That then is our appointment.

– Very good, Father. Six o'clock on the first.

That is how this Father Cobble shuffled gently into Mick's life and affairs, unasked by him. His story about a short holiday was, of course, an improvisation but not, let it be said, anything of panic. He wanted no sudden confrontation with this Jesuit Father for a number of reasons, and straightway felt mildly angry that Mary had committed him this way, showing small feeling for his intellectual integrity. First he would have to tell Hackett and see what he had to say, assuming it would be possible to get him to take the prospect seriously. Secondly, he was anxious to have the facts, and all

63

of them, from Mary about Father Cobble. What sort of a man was he, what age, of what ecclesiastical status and exactly what sort of 'problems' did he advise on? The last point was the most important, he felt. The well-meaning but meddling and obtuse clergyman was often more than a mere nuisance. In questioning and praying to isolate and analyse a visitor's problem (if the latter in fact had a problem) he could grow to be a considerable new problem himself. And Mick reminded himself that while he observed reasonably well the rules of the Church, he had never found himself much in rapport in the human scene with any priest. In the confessional he had often found their queries naïve, stupid, occasionally impertinent; and the feeling that they meant well and were doing their best was merely an additional exasperation. He was complete enough in himself, he thought: educated, tolerant, contemptuous of open vice or licentious language but ever careful to show charity to those who in weakness had stayed. If he had a weakness all his own, it was thoughtless indulgence in alcohol; this dulled moral insight, unbalanced the judgement and – heavens! – could lead the mind to sinful reveries of the carnal kind. With God's help alcohol would soon be put in its place, but not in any sudden silly peremptory gesture. A modulation – adult, urbane, unhurried – was called for.

His mother? It might be thought odd that his poor mother, with whom he lived alone, so little occupied his thoughts. She was simple and devout in the manner of Mrs Laverty but much older. She was indeed an old woman and to talk to her even in the mildest and most superficial way about the like of De Selby was unthinkable; the very idea itself was almost funny. If she understood a word, she would charitably conclude that he had 'a sup taken', for, having loved his father and accepted that he had died from drink, she well knew he was no stranger to the taverns. Yes, it is strange and sad to live so close to one so dear and yet have no real point of contact outside banal and trivial smalltalk, no

64

access to exchanges of the mind. Did he not notice the state nearly all his shirts were getting into? How often must he be reminded to buy at least four pairs of socks? Ah, but it was a sweet dead-end.

He went to a play at the Gaiety. Halfway through he knew he was wasting his time. And the following evening he took a tram to Dalkey. Hackett had no telephone at home or at business and this was the only way of chancing a meeting with him or leaving a message. The light of the Colza looked brighter, though no doubt the candlepower was the same as ever. Even as he pushed the door he could hear Hackett's voice beyond the inner partition. Hackett was elevated in voice and manner when he found him in the 'Slum' with Sergeant Fottrell, though each was separately seated. Behind the bar was Larry, an oldish small grey character who never had much to say, nominally the cellarman but charged with countless chores, from cleaning latrines and grates to watering the plants in pots all over the house upstairs. Hackett nodded to his old friend Mick.

– God bless you and isn't it the sublime and fabulous evening, thanks be to the Lord and His Holy Mother, the sergeant said smiling.

– Good night to you, Sergeant. I must apologize for not yet having called for the bike.

– 'Tis no harm at all boy. I have it imprisoned in a cell without a chance of parole, and I ordered Policeman Pluck to subject it to fastidious oiling about the hubs and levers.

Mick said thanks and asked Larry for a pint.

– I was just telling the Sergeant, said Hackett loudly, about Judas Iscariot. Now *there* was a decent man that was taken in and made a gobshite out of. The unfortunate poor whore was like a man going round with his head in a sack, and maybe drunk.

– He answered for what he did, the same as we all will have to, Mick replied. He found Hackett irked him.

– Now listen here. Don't give me any of that sort of talk at all. I've looked into this whole thing in Marsh's Library. Judas was an intellectual type. He knew what he was doing. Furthermore, he was swindled. He got the worst deal of the lot in the whole shooting match.

– We are not sure what deal he got in the end. Remember De Selby's effort to find out.

– O'Scariot was a man of deciduous character inferentially, Sergeant Fottrell announced.

– We know at least what he did. He got thirty pieces of silver. What sort of pay is that?

– We are not sure of the value of that payment in terms of today.

– Answer the question, man, Hackett pursued hotly. What relationship could that payment bear to the value of what he sold?

– He was a businessman and should himself be a proper judge of value.

– He was shamelessly swindled by those crooks the Pharisees.

Mick was briefly silent, drinking his porter, hoping that Hackett would cool down. He was breaking their agreement, in the presence of the sergeant, to hold their peace. Mick thought to pull the talk to another trend.

– They say he bought a field with the money, he ventured.

– Ah now, interposed the sergeant, I have often thought that that divil of a man was at heart a country Irishman, consecutively because of his eerie love of the sod—

– Hardly, Mick muttered.

– His soft yearning for good parturitional land phlegmatically, with its full desposits of milk and honeysuckle.

– As I said before, Hackett barked savagely, Peter was a worse louser and lackey, perpetrated his low perfidity *after* Judas had betrayed his Master, and got nothing but thanks for his day's work. Yes sir! The Case of the Missing Witness. Judas may have had a good and honourable intention, as De

Quincey held. Peter's conduct was mean and cowardly, his first concern being his own skin. Yes, that's one thing I'm going to work for.

– What?'

– Rehabilitating Judas Iscariot.

– He was the class of a man, the sergeant put in, that you would meet exactly in a place like Swanlinbar, or in Cushendun of a fair day.

– How will you do that?

– Agitate to have the record amended. All the obloquy heaped on him is based on nothing but inference. I hope to have part of the Bible re-written.

– The Holy Father would have a say in that.

– To hell with the Holy Father. I will work to secure that the Bible contains the Gospel according to Saint Judas.

– Saint Judas, pray for us, the sergeant recited solemnly, then drank solemnly.

Hackett glared at him, then turned on Mick.

– Who better than Judas could tell the inner truth and declare what his intentions were – his plan?

– The historicity of the existing Gospels, he explained, is not seriously disputed anywhere. It is equally accepted that Judas left no record. You ask who but Judas could tell the inner truth? Perhaps. But he didn't. He told nothing.

Hackett's features were arranged in a deep sneer.

– For a learned and enlightened man, you are surely a buck ignoramus. The Roman Church's Bible has a great lot of material named Apocrypha. There have been apocryphal Gospels according to Peter, Thomas, Barnabas, John, Judas Iscariot and many others. My task would be to retrieve, clarify and establish the Iscariot Gospel.

– Suppose you did find an historically plausible testament and then found Judas saying something you didn't expect at all, something dead contrary to your argument?

– Don't be more of a poor bastard than you can help.

Mick poured the rest of the pint down the inside of his

neck and replaced the tumbler on the counter with finality.

– My decision, he announced, is to buy a glawsheen of whiskey for you two gentlemen and another pint for myself. Larry, please do the needful in the cause of peace.

– Isn't that most timely and herbaceous? the sergeant remarked genially. Hackett frowned but seemed a bit mollified, perhaps thinking that his talk had been too emphatic and should not be pursued. Mick hoped he could get through to his real mission.

– I want to tell you about something, he said as Larry hurried about his task. Somebody I mentioned De Selby to has accidentally taken a slightly embarrassing step without my knowledge.

Hackett stared at him glumly.

– I think I know who the somebody is, he growled. What has she done?

– Well, it was her mother. She arranged for a Jesuit to see me.

A what? A *Jesuit*?

– Yes. But apparently this Father Cobble from Milltown knows nothing yet except that somebody's in trouble. And personally I know nothing of Father Cobble and haven't yet been able to find out. The meeting has been provisionally arranged for this day week at the Royal Marine.

– Well sweet God, why start messing about with those nosey interfering gobhawks?

– It wasn't *my* idea, I told you. But what do you think of my meeting him, giving him a very brief account, a rough outline, of De Selby and then inviting him to come up the Vico with me to visit him?

Hackett grimaced, laughed mirthlessly, and savoured his new drink.

– Be clear at the outset, he said, that I won't be present. That would be too much. De Selby might push out the boat and arrange a high-class dinner party to welcome this priest. Chief guests John the Baptist, Jerome, the Little Flower,

68

Saint Thomas à Kempis, Matt Talbot, the four "Saint Patricks, and Saint Joan.

– But what do you think? Be serious.

– If your idea is to simplify the descent of Augustine, I think you would be going the right way about complicating it. The matter might be referred to Rome, and then where were we? We might be excommunicated.

This attitude was roughly what Mick had expected. But his mind was already made up. Hackett would have been no addition to the little tea-party, anyway.

– I don't agree, he replied, because Jesuits are intelligent and trained men, whatever else they may be. But even complication would be preferable to permanent mystery with no bottom to it. You don't deny that both of us are very puzzled about that early Sunday swim of ours. Those men are bound to have some experience of diabolism, if that is what is in question here. We can't let a matter like this just rest and forget about it.

– I can.

– Yes. You have a mind and courage much superior to what I have. Both of us heard De Selby's threat to destroy all mankind, and both of us were witnesses of his possession of a unique instrument of destruction. To sit and do nothing would be, well . . . inhuman.

– We were not witness of his possession of a unique weapon of destruction. He certainly has an impressive gadget, or chemical, or drug. He destroyed nothing.

– He destroyed the atmosphere and annihilated time as we understand it – exactly as he predicted he would.

– You magnify what are mere impressions and you give yourself a status of grandeur. You know what happened to one Redeemer of humanity. Do you want to be another?

– I'm determined to do something, and the Father Cobble suggestion is as good as any, though it's not my own.

– As you please.

— Lawrence of Arabian sands, chanted Sergeant Fottrell, be at my back insidiously and replenish the beakers of the company continentally.

— Thanks, Sergeant, Hackett said casually.

— And furthermore, Mick continued, after this drink I am going to see De Selby, and ask him will he receive the reverend Father.

And he did, alone.

8

Mick was startled at the promptness with which the door was opened after a knock, as if De Selby had been waiting behind it after having been warned of an approaching visitor by supernatural telephone. There he stood, smiling primly and bidding welcome. He led the way, not into the room of the previous visit but to a smaller apartment at the back which, for its shelves and cases of bottles and jars, electrical apparatus, crucibles, scales, measuring vessels and all the conventional paraphernalia of scientific experiment, one must call a laboratory. There were however at the empty fireplace a few comfortable chairs and a small chess table. He took Mick's hat and from somewhere behind him produced a bottle and two glasses.

— You'll forgive me saying it, Michael, he remarked as he sat down, but I'm glad your companion is not with you. I found him rather superficial.

This rather dismayed Mick, for De Selby's manners hitherto had been pretty faultless. But he showed no sign.

— Ah well he's a bit hasty and thoughtless sometimes, he replied. Glad I caught you at home. May I ask whether you have had any further, em . . . spiritual experiences since, sub aqua or otherwise?

De Selby had risen and carefully poured out two drinks.

– Oh yes. More wide-ranging but not so illuminating. Old Testament characters tend to be simple, ignorant and superstitious compared with those Christian sophists, heresiarchs and mendacious early Fathers.

– Indeed? Whom did you speak to, if I may ask?

– Two of the boyos, separately. Jonas was one of them, or Jonah as the Protestants call him. Why do those untutored blatherskites insist so much on being trivially different?

– Jonas? The man who was swallowed by a whale?

– The proper answer to that is yes and no, though you are on the right track. I personally don't believe it was a whale. In old times the shark was an immense creature, up to ninety feet in length.

– Does it matter much whether it was a whale or a shark?

– It does to me in my office as theologian. The references in the Bible, in Testaments Old and New, are consistently to 'a great fish'. The whale as such is never mentioned, and in any event the whale is not a fish. Scientists hold, with ample documentation in support, that the whale was formerly a land animal, its organs now modified for sea-living. It is a mammal, suckles its young, is warm-blooded and must come to the surface for breath, like man himself. It is most unlikely that there were any whales in the sea in the time of Jonas.

– You surprise me, Mr De Selby. The belief that it was a whale is pretty universal.

– That may be, but the creature has been the subject of much casuistry, no doubt stimulated by the Jesuits. Its flesh is quite edible, like the dolphin's. Roman Catholics are forbidden, as we know, to eat fleshmeat on Fridays. But on those days they have not hesitated to eat whale, on the specious ground that it is a fish. It is not a fish even in its mode of propulsion, which is by its tail. A whale's great tail is horizontal whereas the tail of absolutely every real fish is vertical.

– Well, well. You seem to be well versed also in what I will call natural piscine philosophy.

– Oh, now now. Another point is that the shark is piscivorous, whereas the whale subsists almost exclusively on plankton, which one might describe as minute marine vegetables.

This discourse did in fact impress Mick, maybe because his personal Bible studies had been as minute as plankton. Apparently little was outside the range of De Selby's reading or meditation.

– Tell me, Mick ventured, had Jonas himself any idea about the true identity of his . . . host?

Here De Selby swallowed a long slow trickle of his peerless *hausgemacht*, and paused before replying.

– To tell you the truth, Michael, I found Jonas to be a bit of a ballocks.

– *What*? Not only the word itself but the sinister fervour of its pronunciation was like a slap in the face to Mick – and earnest, perhaps, of an innocence he did not know he had.

– And the Lord was also of the same opinion.

– But Jonas was a prophet, wasn't he?

– He was a prophet who disgraced himself. He disobeyed God's orders because, muryaa, he knew better. That's why he was heaved into the sea.

– How did he disobey?

– He was commanded by the Lord to go and preach in the great and evil city of Nineveh. But he knew better than the Lord, knew that the people would repent and reform, that going there was a waste of time, and instead took ship to go elsewhere. A frightful storm arose, the Lord's punishment for Jonas, and the crew, knowing their lives were all in danger because of him, threw him into the sea. The storm immediately died down but meanwhile for Jonas Mr Shark arrived.

– Well, that's what I asked. Did Jonas give any evidence to justify your choice of a shark?

– The Bible merely says that he spent three days and nights

in the *belly* of the creature. Not clear how anybody could distinguish night from day in the darkness.

– Perhaps hunger would be a guide?

– If 'belly' means 'stomach', there's a big difference between the belly of a shark and that of a whale. A whale's stomach is like a house or a flat – it has several compartments. You could have a dining-room there, a bedroom, a kitchen, perhaps a library.

– But you talked to Jonas. Did he make any remark himself about the inside of the monster that gobbled him?

– Not at all. He talked bull, like a cheap politician or a first-year Jesuit novice.

– That was disappointing.

– Well, he was eventually vomited up on dry land. We can't expect the victims of miracles to explain the miracles. Besides, several of those old-time prophets were mouthpieces in the pejorative American meaning.

They drank in silence, pondering this strange occurrence, the dark mystery infixed in it, unresolved even by a consultation between De Selby and Jonas himself; very strange indeed. But who was De Selby's second colloquist, Mick wondered, as another generous drink was poured for him. Saint Teresa of Avila?

Who was the subject of your second interview, Mr De Selby?

– Ah yes. Francis of Assisi, of course, founder of the Franciscans. A strange man. Like Ignatius of Loyola, his early life was profligate and deplorable, and again like him, he saw the truth in the course of a dangerous illness. But Francis was a genuine saint, and a poet, too.

– Funny thing, Mick responded, I recently met another poet myself – in the Colza Hotel, of all places. A chap by the name of Nemo Crabbe. He is doing medicine against his will at Trinity but refuses to live in the College because every student has to empty his own charley.

De Selby blinked a little in surprise.

– Dear me, he said mildly, do they not have servants there, or houseboys?
– Apparently not. Was your interview with Saint Francis important?

De Selby paused in recollection.

– Of only middling importance. He was very honest and did little more than verify what is now received knowledge about him. I told him his canonization only two years after his death was hasty and presumptuous. He bluntly told me to make that complaint to Gregory the Ninth.
– Is it true that he preached to the birds, and all that kind of thing?
– Possibly not literally but as a man he was most gentle and kind to all kind creatures, seeing nothing but God's handi-work all about him. He could perhaps be faulted for a streak of pantheism.
– Yes. I do not know much about him except that he and the birds appear so often on calendars at Christmas.
– Oh he was the genuine article and not a trick-of-the-loop merchant like Augustine. He totally lacked arrogance. And he did receive the Stigmata of the Crucified after a fast of forty days on a mountain. But the poor fellow was very shy about that . . .

De Selby chuckled genially.

– He seemed to blush at the mention of it as if I was com-plimenting a schoolboy on winning the hundred yards dash.

They paused in their talk from these two sacred con-ferences to a general survey of De Selby's ghastly plan for world catastrophe. Mick asked him did he not find the known world of the common man, lit up and shot through with the magic of the preternatural world to which he had access, far too absorbing and wonderful an organized cre-ation to be destroyed summarily and utterly? He grew stern at the mention of such themes. No, this globe only was in question and the destruction he planned was a prescribed doom, terrible but ineluctable, and a duty before God so far as he personally was concerned. The whole world was corrupt, human society an insufferable abomination. God had founded his own true Church but contemplated benevolently the cults of even capricious dæmons provided they were intrinsically good. Christianity is God's religion but Judaism, Buddhism, Hinduism and Islam are tolerable manifestations of God; the Old and New Testaments, the Veda, Koran and Avesta are all sacred documents but in fact every one of those organized religions were in decomposition and atrophy. The Almighty had led De Selby to the D.M.P. substance so that the Supreme Truth could be protected finally and irrevocably from all the Churches of today.

– In fact, Mick asked, is this a second divine plan for the salvation of mankind?

– You could call it that.

– Salvation by way of complete destruction?

– There is no other way. All will be called home and judged.

Mick did not feel like pursuing such colloquy. Though somewhat shielded by the gentle fumes of his host's whiskey, his mind felt sickeningly clouded by the modest claim of De Selby – for it was nothing less – that he was in fact a new Messiah. Mick thought: what blasphemous drollery! Yet . . . D.M.P. did exist. He knew that, so did Hackett. Oh, hells bells!

He remembered the errand that brought him and suddenly he was not shy or hesitant at all in mentioning Father Cobble; in fact he was relieved in recalling the good priest, and gladly enough he accepted another drink – but a small one.

– Mr De Selby, he said, please do not think I wish to heap you with vulgar flattery but I honestly do find your remarks on comparative religions, theocracy and the final imponderables of physical death and eternity fascinating.

– Eschatology has always attracted the minds of men who use reason.

– Well, talking of Churches, there's an old friend of mine, Father Cobble . . .

75

– Father Cobble? What a name! I know a Father Stone, a Cistercian.

– Easy, Mr De Selby. Father Cobble's a Jesuit.

– Ah – *ignatius elenchi*! What fine friends you have, Michael.

– Actually he is a most intelligent man. He could give you an argument, I'll bet. He knows all about philosophy and Church history.

– I don't doubt that, for the Jesuits are well set-up chaps in their own business – or think they are.

– Would you be annoyed if I brought him along for an evening on the first of next month? He's excellent company – that I'll guarantee.

De Selby laughed genuinely and deeply, and topped up the drinks with a little water.

– Of course bring him up, he smiled. Cultured company is one thing I conspicuously lack in this house, though privacy, alas, is essential most of the time for my work. You understand that, I know. But that does not mean that I have to live in solitary confinement. But tell me one thing, Michael.

– Certainly. What is that?

– Is the reverence partial to a glass of good whiskey or does he go for the red wine?

A nice question, about a man he'd never even met.

– I . . . I'm not sure. Our meetings have always been on neutral ground.

– Never mind. There's plenty of wine here, though not home-made.

Thus was the bargain arranged. But it was at least an hour later when Mick shook hands with De Selby at his door. His talk had suddenly veered into native politics and here at last was terrain where he was uncertain and sometimes lost, but where Mick was the very experienced guide.

9

The old coloured houses of irregular size along the narrow quays of the Liffey seem to lean outward as if to study themselves in the water; but on his pleasant walk there this time, Mick's eye was not dwelling pleasurably on them. He was thinking, though not in gloom. There had come to him an idea that seemed bright, masterly, bold even. True, it would not dissipate the underwater ghost of Augustine nor extinguish the neuro-psychotic aberrations of De Selby but he became convinced it would enable him *to do something* to prevent, perhaps permanently but certainly for the present, the carrying out of any genuine plan to visit the human race with havoc. He was pleased. He resolved to go to a quiet place where alcoholic drinks were to be had and then, please God, not have one but try something healthy, refreshing, harmless. Plain thinking – planning – was called for.

And Father Cobble? Yes, Mick would keep that arrangement to bring him on a visit to De Selby. The visit might well be valuable and, also, he was glad that Hackett had reneged. He felt Hackett's presence might have been a complication, even an obstacle, and this was also true of the steps he would have to take later to give effect to his new idea.

His steps led him to the Metropole in Dublin's main street. It was not called a cinema, restaurant, dance hall or drinking den, though it contained all of these delights. Drinking was done in a quiet, softly-lighted lounge downstairs where tables were sequestered by tall fixed screens of dark wood. It was a favourite resort of parish priests from the country and, though service was by waitresses, lady customers were excluded.

He sat down and ordered a small Vichy water. When another order had been served in the division next to him he was sharply startled by the unseen customer's thanks, unmistakable in content if not in tone.

– In gratitude for that bottle, me dear colleen, I will make a novena for the implenishment of your soul irreciprocally to Saint Martin of Tours himself.

No help for it: Mick picked up his drink and moved in. Happily, Sergeant Fottrell was alone. In old-fashioned courtesy he stood up and put out a hand.

– Well, the Lord forbid but you must be following me detectively?

Mick laughed.

– No indeed. I wanted a quiet drink and thought nobody would know me down here.

– Ah, but the divil minds his own children.

Curiously, this unscheduled collision with the Sergeant did not seem to erode Mick's half-formed desire to be by himself. In fact he was glad to see the sergeant. He apologized once more for having failed to retrieve his bicycle from the station in Dalkey. The Sergeant took his long upper lip from his glass of barley wine with a wince of total absolution.

– Where the bicycle is, he said gravely, is a far safer place than the high highroad itself, intuitively.

– Oh, I just thought it might be in the way.

– It is under lock and key in cell number two and you are far better in your health to be divorced from it. Tell me this item: how did you find Policeman Pluck?

– I had met him before, of course. A very pleasant man.

– What was he doing perceptively?

– He was busy mending a puncture.

– Ah-ha!

The sergeant sniggered, took another sup from his drink and frowned slightly in thought.

– That will be the third puncture in seven days, he said, in what seemed to be a tone of satisfaction.

– That looks a pretty awful record, Mick replied. Is it sheer bad luck or is it the bad roads?

– 'Tis the Council must take the credit for the little back roads, the worst in Ireland. But Policeman Pluck got his punctures at half one on Monday, two o'clock on Wednesday, and half six on Sunday.

– How on earth do you know that? Does he keep a diary of them?

– He does not. I know the dates and times protruberantly because it was my good self who carried out the punctures with my penknife.

– Good heavens, why?

– For Policeman Pluck's good luck. But sitting here I have been considering meditatively those talking pictures upstairs. They are a quaint achievious science certainly.

– They are a great advance on silent films.

– You know how they are worked?

– Oh yes. The photo-electric cell.

– Yes then. Why if you can turn light into sound you cannot turn sound into light?

– You mean invent a *phono*-electric cell?

– Of a particular certainty, but for sure that invention would be a hard pancake. I do often contemplate what sort of a light the noble American Constitution would make, given out by President Roosevelt.

– A very interesting speculation.

– Or a speech by Arthur Griffith?

– Yes indeed.

– Charles Stewart Parnell held the dear belief that all Ireland's woes and tears were the true result of being so fond of green. Wrap the green flag round me, boys. If you put that grand man's speeches through the cell (and many a month he spent in a cell himself) wouldn't it be the hemochromic thing if the solution was a bright green light?

Mick laughed at this, and at the whole wonderful idea. There had been, he seemed to remember, an organ that 'played' light on a screen, enchanting patterns of mixes and colour. But that was not what the sergeant had conceived.

– Yes. And that would be the colour of Caruso's voice, or John McCormack singing *Down by the Sally Gardens*? But

79

tell me, Sergeant. Why did you persistently puncture Policeman Pluck's tyres?

The sergeant beckoned the waitress, ordered a barley wine for himself and a small bottle of 'that' for his friend. Then he leaned forward confidentially.

– Did you ever discover or hear tell of mollycules? he asked.

– I did of course.

– Would it surprise or collapse you to know that the Mollycule Theory is at work in the parish of Dalkey?

– Well . . . yes and no.

– It is doing terrible destruction, he continued, the half of the people is suffering from it, it is worse than the small-pox.

– Could it not be taken in hand by the Dispensary Doctor or the National Teachers, or do you think it is a matter for the head of the family?

– The lock, stock and barrel of it all, he replied almost fiercely, is the County Council.

– It seems a complicated thing all right.

The sergeant drank delicately, deep in thought.

– Michael Gilhaney, a man I know, he said finally, is an example of a man that is nearly banjaxed from the operation of the Mollycule Theory. Would it astonish you ominously to hear that he is in danger of being a bicycle?

Mick shook his head in polite incomprehension.

– He is nearly sixty years of age by plain computation, the Sergeant said, and if he is itself, he has spent no less than thirty-five years riding his bicycle over the rocky roadsteads and up and down the pertimious hills and into the deep ditches when the road goes astray in the strain of the winter. He is always going to a particular destination or other on his bicycle at every hour of the day or coming back from there at every other hour. If it wasn't that his bicycle was stolen every Monday he would be sure to be more than halfway now.

– Halfway to where?

– Halfway to being a bloody bicycle himself.

'Had Sergeant Fottrell for once betrayed himself into drunken rambling? His fancies were usually amusing but not so good when they were meaningless. When Mick said something of the kind the Sergeant stared at him impatiently.

– Did you ever study the Mollycule Theory when you were a lad? he asked. Mick said no, not in any detail.

– That is a very serious defalcation and an abstruse exacerbation, he said severely, but I'll tell you the size of it. Everything is composed of small mollycules of itself and they are flying around in concentric circles and arcs and segments and innumerable various other routes too numerous to mention collectively, never standing still or resting but spinning away and darting hither and thither and back again, all the time on the go. Do you follow me intelligently? Mollycules?

– I think I do.

– They are as lively as twenty punky leprechauns doing a jig on the top of a flat tombstone. Now take a sheep. What is a sheep only millions of little bits of sheepness whirling around doing intricate convulsions inside the baste. What else is it but that?

– That would be bound to make the sheep dizzy, Mick observed, especially if the whirling was going on inside the head as well.

The sergeant gave him a look which no doubt he himself would describe as one of non-possum and noli-me-tangere.

– That's a most foolhardy remark, he said sharply, because the nerve-strings and the sheep's head itself are whirling into the same bargain and you can cancel out one whirl against the other and there you are – like simplifying a division sum when you have fives above and below the bar.

– To say the truth I did not think of that.

– Mollycules is a very intricate theorem and can be worked out with algebra but you would want to take it by degrees with rulers and cosines and familiar other instruments and then at the wind-up not believe what you had proved at all. If that happened you would have to go back over it till you

81

got a place where you could believe your own facts and figures as exactly delineated from Hall and Knight's Algebra and then go on again from that particular place till you had the whole pancake properly believed and not have bits of it half-believed or a doubt in your head hurting you like when you lose the stud of your shirt in the middle of the bed.

– Very true, Mick decided to say.

– If you hit a rock hard enough and often enough with an iron hammer, some mollycules of the rock will go into the hammer and contrariwise likewise.

– That is well known, he agreed.

– The gross and net result of it is that people who spend most of their natural lives riding iron bicycles over the rocky roadsteads of the parish get their personalities mixed up with the personalities of their bicycles as a result of the interchanging of the mollycules of each of them, and you would be surprised at the number of people in country parts who are nearly half people and half bicycles.

Mick made a little gasp of astonishment that made a sound like the air coming from a bad puncture.

– Good Lord, I suppose you're right.

– And you would be unutterably flibbergasted if you knew the number of stout bicycles that partake serenely of humanity.

Here the sergeant produced his pipe, a thing he did very rarely in public, and in silence commenced the laborious business of filling and ramming it from his battered tin of very dark tobacco. Mick began to muse and think of country places he had known in his younger days. He thought of one place he had been fond of.

Brown bogs and black bogs were neatly arranged on each side of the road with rectangular boxes carved out of them here and there, each with a filling of yellow-brown brown-yellow water. Far away near the sky tiny people were stooped at their turf-work, cutting out precisely-shaped sods with their patent spades and building them into a tall memorial the height of a horse and cart. Sounds came from them, delivered to his ears without charge by the west wind, sounds of laughing and whistling and bits of verses from the old bog-songs. Nearer, a house stood attended by three trees and surrounded by the happiness of a coterie of fowls, all of them picking and rooting and disputating loudly in the unrelenting manufacture of their eggs. The house was quiet in itself and silent but a canopy of lazy smoke had been erected over the chimney to indicate that people were within engaged on tasks. Ahead of him went the road, running swiftly across the flat land and pausing slightly to climb slowly up a hill that was waiting for it in a place where there was tall grass, grey boulders and rank stunted trees. The whole overhead was occupied by the sky, translucent, impenetrable, ineffable and incomparable, with a fine island of cloud anchored in the calm two yards to the right of Mr Jarvis's outhouse.

The scene was real and incontrovertible but at variance with the talk of the sergeant. Was it not monstrous to allege that the little people winning turf far away were partly bicycles? He took a sideways view of him. He had now compacted his turf-like tobacco and produced a box of matches.

– Are you sure about the humanity of bicycles? Mick enquired of him. Does it not go against the doctrine of original sin? Or is the Molecule Theory as dangerous as you say?

The sergeant was drawing fiercely at the pipe as his match spluttered.

– It is between twice and three times as dangerous as it might be, he replied gloomily. Early in the morning I often think it is four times and, for goodness' sake, if you lived here for a few days and gave full and free rein to your observation and inspection, you would know how certain the sureness of the certainty is.

– Policeman Pluck did not look like a bicycle, Mick said. He had no back wheel on him and hadn't so much as a bell on his right thumb.

The sergeant looked at him with some commiseration.

– You cannot expect him to grow handlebars out of his neck but I have seen him attempt things more acutely indescribable than that. Did you ever notice the queer behaviour of bicycles in the country, or the more-man-bicycles?

– I did not.

– It's an indigenous catastrophe. When a man lets things go too far, you will not see much because he spends a lot of time leaning with one elbow on walls or standing propped up by one foot at the path. Such a man is a futile phenomenon of great charm and intensity and a very dangerous article.

– Dangerous to other people, you mean?

– Dangerous to himself and everybody. I once knew a man named Doyle. He was thirty-one per cent.

– Well, that's not too serious.

The sergeant was puffing industriously, his pipe now in fine order.

– Maybe. You can thank me. There were three Doyle brothers in the house and they were too contemptuously poor to have a bicycle apiece. Some people never know how fortunate they are when they are poorer than each other. But bedamn but one of the brothers won a prize of ten pounds in *John Bull.* When I got precise wind of this tiding I knew I would have to take quick steps unless there was to be two new bicycles in the family, because you will understand that I can steal only a limited number of bicycles in a month. Luckily I knew the postman well and I gave him a talking-to to divert the cheque to myself. The postman! Ah, great, sweet, brown stirabout!

Recollection of this public servant seemed to move the sergeant to sad sardonic chuckles, with intricate gesturings of his red hands.

– The postman? Mick asked.

– Seventy-two per cent, he said quietly.

– Great Lord!

– A round of twenty-nine miles on the bicycle every single

day for forty years, hail, rain or snowballs. There was very little hope of getting his number down below fifty again. I got him to cash the cheque in a private sub-office and we split the money in the public interest paternalistically.

Funny thing, Mick did not feel that the sergeant had been dishonest; he had been sentimental, rather, and the state of the postman meant that no moral issue was involved.

He asked the sergeant how the bicycle, for its part, would behave from day to day in a situation like this.

– The behaviour of a bicycle with a very high content of *homo sapiens*, he explained, is very cunning and entirely remarkable. You never see them moving by themselves but you meet them in the least accountable of places unexpectedly. Did you ever see a bicycle leaning against the dresser in a warm kitchen when it is pouring outside?

– I did.

– Not very far from the fire?

– Yes.

– Near enough to the family to hear the conversation?

– I suppose so.

– Not a thousand miles from where they keep the eatables?

– I did not notice that. Good Lord, you do not mean to say that these bicycles *eat food*?

– They were never seen doing it, nobody ever caught them with a mouthful of seedy cake. All I know is that food disappears.

– What!

– It is not the first time I have noticed crumbs at the front wheels of some of those gentlemen.

Rather feebly Mick gestured to the waitress and ordered another drink. The Sergeant was in deadly earnest, no doubt about that. And this was the man Mick had decided to call in to help him in resolving the great St Augustine enigma. He felt strangely depressed.

– Nobody takes any notice, the Sergeant said softly. Tom thinks that Pat is responsible for missing grubsteaks, and Pat thinks that Tom is instrumental. Very few of the people guess what is going on in such a fearsomely infractional house. There are other things, too . . . but it's better not to talk of them.

– Oh come now, Sergeant. What sort of other things?

– Well, a man riding a lady's bicycle. It's the height of sulphurous immorality, the P.P. would be within his rights in forbidding such a low character put as much as his nose inside the church.

– Yes . . . such conduct is unseemly.

– God help the nation that weakens on such matters. You would have bicycles demanding votes, and they would look for seats on the County Council to make the roads far worse than they are for their own ulterior motivation. But against that and on the other hand, a good bicycle is a great companion, a friend, there is great charm about it.

– All the same, I doubt if I'll ever again get up on that bicycle of mine you have in the station out in Dalkey.

The sergeant shook his head genially.

– Ah now, a little of it is a good thing, it makes you hardy and puts iron into you. But shure walking too far too often too quickly isn't safe at all either. The cracking of your feet on the road makes a certain amount of road come up into you. When a man dies they say he returns to clay funereally but too much walking fills you up with clay far sooner (or buries bits of you along the road) and brings your death halfway to meet you. It is not easy to know fastidiously what is the best way to move yourself from one place to another.

There was a little silence. Mick thought of mentioning how intact one could remain by restricting oneself to air travel but decided not to; the sergeant would surely object on the ground of cost. Mick noticed his face had become clouded and that he was staring into the bowl of his pipe.

– I will tell you a secret confidentially, he said in a low voice. My own grandfather was eighty-three when we buried him. For five years before his death he was a horse.

– *A horse?*

– A horse in everything but extraneous externalities, because he had spent years of his life – far too many for safety, be the pipers – in the saddle. Usually he was lazy and quiet but now and again he would go for a smart gallop, clearing the hedges in great style. Did you ever see a man on two legs galloping?

– I did not.

– Well, I am given to understand it is a great sight. He always said he won the Grand National when he was a lot younger and used to annoy the life out of his family with stories about the intricate jumps and the insoluble tallness of them.

– And the grandfather got himself into this condition by too much horse-riding?

– That was the size of it. His old horse Dan was in the contrary way of thinking and gave so much trouble, coming into the house at night, interfering with young girls during the day and committing indictable offences, that they had to shoot him. The polis of the time was not sympathetic exiguously. They said they would have to arrest the horse and have him up at the next Petty Sessions unless he was done away with. So the family shot him but if you ask me it was my grandfather they shot and it is the horse that is buried in Cloncoonla churchyard.

The sergeant fell to musing on his complicated ancestry but had the presence of mind to beckon the waitress with his pipe and order a repeat dose of the quiet medicine.

– In a way, Mick observed, your grandfather's case was not so bad. I mean, a horse is at least a creature, a living thing, man's companion on earth and indeed he is accounted everywhere a noble animal. Now, if it was a pig . . .

The sergeant turned and beamed on him, and gave a long contented puff at his pipe.

– You say that from a good heart, and it is subsidiary and solemn of you. The Irish people have great graw for the horse. When Tipperary Tim died, the cabhorse that won the Grand National and the only one of the whole field left standing, be the holy God you'd swear it was a beloved Archbishop that had gone to his eternal reward. Strong men was seen crying.

– Yes, and think of Orby, the great horse that won the National for Boss Croker. To this day he lies there at Sandyford.

– Ah yes. And then there was Master McGrath, the dog that was faster than the wind. A statue of him stands at a crossroads down in Tipp. where the mother comes from.

Both of them pleasurably savoured their kinship with the higher animals, though personally Mick drew the line at becoming one of them by a process of prolonged carnal intercussion.

– Well, Sergeant, I am delighted that we are quite agreed on one thing at least. Human metamorphosis vis-à-vis an iron bicycle is quite another matter. And there is more to it than the monstrous exchange of tissue for metal.

– And what would that be? the sergeant asked curiously.

– All decent Irishmen should have a proper national outlook. Practically any bike you have in Ireland was made in either Birmingham or Coventry.

– I see the point intimately. Yes. There is also an element of treason entailed. Quite right.

It seemed that this point had never occurred to him and a frown gathered about him as he inwardly considered it, puffing stolidly and compacting the tobacco in his bowl with a well-charred finger.

– Oh, now, he said at last, faith and the bicycle is no hilarity of itself as a gigantic social problem. In me younger days it led to a hanging.

– Is that so?

– It did bedad. I was stationed in Borrisokane at the time and there was a very famous man there be the name of McDadd. McDadd held the national record for the hundred

88

miles on the solid tyre. I need not tell you with exactitude what the solid tyre did for him. We had to hang the bicycle.

– Hang the bicycle?

– McDadd had a first-class grudge against another man named MacDonaghy but he did not go near MacDonaghy. He knew how things stood there, and he gave Mac-Donaghy's bicycle a ferocious thrashing with a crowbar. After that McDadd and MacDonaghy had a fast fist fight and MacDonaghy – a dark man with glasses – did not live to know who the winner was.

– Well, wouldn't that be a case of manslaughter?

– Not with the sergeant we had in them days. He held it was murder most foul and a bad case of criminality into the same bargain. We couldn't find McDadd for a long time or make sure where the most of him was. We had to arrest his bicycle as well as himself and we minutely watched the two of them under secret observation for a week to see where the majority of McDadd was and whether the bicycle was mostly in McDadd's backside *pari passu* and vice versa if you understand my meaning.

– I think I do, but I can also see the possibility of a charge of conspiracy.

– Maybe so, maybe not. The sergeant gave his ruling at the end of the week. His position was painful in the extremity of pain because he was a close friend of McDadd after office hours. He condemned the bicycle and it was the bicycle that was hanged.

It seemed to Mick a very summary form of justice, and apparently the sentence had been imposed and carried out without the formality of court proceedings.

– I think that perhaps there was a miscarriage of the carriageway there, he commented.

– They were rough days, the sergeant replied, smoking thoughtfully. But there was a great wake afterwards, and the bicycle was buried in the same grave as MacDonaghy. Did you ever see a bicycle-shaped-coffin?

– No.

– It is a very inconvoluted item of wood-working, you would want to be a master-class carpenter to make a good job of the handlebars, to say nothing of the pedals and the backstep.

– I don't doubt that.

– Ah yes. The days of racing on the solid tyre were sad days for Ireland.

The sergeant fell silent again. One could almost hear the gentle wash of the tide of memory in his head.

– There were tragedic cases, too, of another kind entirely. I remember an old man. He was harmless enough but he had the people driven loopy by the queer way he moved and walked. He'd go up a little gentle hill at a speed of maybe half a mile an hour but at other times he would run so fast that you'd swear he was doing up to fifteen emm pee aitch. And that's a fact by damn.

– Did anybody find out what was wrong with him?

– One very intelligent, perspicuous and infractious man did. It was meself. Do you know what was wrong with the poor bugger?

– No. What?

– He was suffering severely from Sturmey Archer. He was the first in the country to fit the three-speed gear at the turn of the century.

– Yes, I think I can see the various possible complications. For instance, I think racing bikes have forks with special springing in them. Yes. It's all very interesting. But now, I promised to be home early and I'm going to buy a final drink.

Mick beckoned the waitress.

– I want to ask you about something, he added.

As the drinks were coming he bethought himself, as they say in the old books. He had enjoyed the sergeant's per-oration and his abstruse subject. It would be fitting, perhaps, to call him the poor man's De Selby. But the latter was still his preoccupation – perhaps he should say his night-and-day obsession. Yet he had a plan now, one that was at once ingenious and daring. He thought it would be only wise and judicious to have the sergeant participate unwittingly in it, for if he were to find certain things out afterwards of his own motion, his undoubted gift for the maladroit could in the end wreck the scheme. Mick had already in his mind assigned a part – again an unwitting one – to Hackett. The date and timing of the operation depended now on one thing only: finding out how De Selby proposed to circulate his deadly D.M.P. substance simultaneously all over the world so as to obviate the condition of insulation, the sort of seal that had obtained in the case of the submarine cavern at Dalkey.

He was not clear how he could do this in a reasonably short time, and prolonged twisting and turning of his own brain yielded no guess about how this mighty task could be accomplished. Even a world Power with tens of thousands of aeroplanes would be daunted by such an undertaking and, supernatural as De Selby's contacts seemed to be, it was doubtful indeed if flights of angels could be invoked. In fact there was no proof that the Almighty approved of De Selby at all. God might be on Mick's side.

– Sergeant Fottrell, he said seriously, I suppose you know Mr De Selby of the Vico Road?

A gentle frown gathered on the face.

– An exemplary and august personality, he replied, but a whit contumacious.

That was promising: respect leavened with suspicion.

– Exactly. I know him rather well myself but he has me worried. In that house of his in the woods he has been carrying out experiments. He is a scientist, of course.

– Ah yes. Piercing insentiently the dim secrets of the holy world.

– Now I am not saying that he is breaking the law. But I do know that he is endangering the community. He does not know, and probably could not be persuaded, that his experiments might get out of control and visit us all with an epidemic of appalling disease, with goodness knows how many people dying like flies and passing on the pestilence to other people as they do so; not only here in Dublin and Dalkey but possibly in England and other parts of the world.

The sergeant had rekindled his pipe.

– That is a most unfavourable and incontinent tiding, he said. That is worse than the question of the bicycles.

– I'm glad you look at it in that way. You are a man, Sergeant, who is bigger than his job, otherwise you would not have stolen bicycles to curtail the deadly cycling of afflicted parties and indeed deliberately puncturing Policeman Pluck's machine.

This speech obviously pleased the sergeant, as Mick intended it would.

– There are times, he said, when I must take my superior officer to be the Man Above. It is my plain duty to guard members of the human race, sometimes from themselves. Not everybody understands the far from scrutable periculums of the intricate world.

– I quite agree. Now I happen to know that Mr De Selby had been artificially incubating the bacteria which cause typhoid fever in humans. Typhoid is a very serious and dangerous disease, even worse than typhus.

– An insatiable importunity.

– Yes.

– An indiscriminate exacerbation much to be inveighed against meticulously.

– Mr De Selby has tens of millions of those microbes in a metal container like a little keg. He has it in his house, locked in a safe.

-- A safe, faith?

– Yes. In the interest of humanity I plan to carry off this container of dangerous bugs away from the scientist's house – steal it if you will – and put it in some safe place where it will do no harm.

– Ah! Well now! Steal it? Yes indeed. I would consider that not contumelious or derogatory.

– Then I can rely, Sergeant, on your co-operation?

He was now relaxed, apparently relieved that the project was no more than to take away something which was, while dangerous, of no monetary value.

– Not only my co-operation but my active condonement of the *res ipsa.* But locked in a safe? I do not know the skills of poking a safe's lock.

– Nor do I. And blowing it up or using force would be very dangerous. But that sort of hazard does not arise at all. The safe looks massive and strong but it is old-fashioned. Look at this!

From a small inside pocket of his jacket Mick extracted a key and held it up.

– I've told you, Sergeant, that our friend is careless, he said, and perhaps I should have said criminally careless and quite reckless. This is the key of the safe. I picked it up from the floor of his sitting-room on a recent visit.

– Well great cripes, the sergeant cried blankly.

– Our task is really simple enough, Mick continued. First we must see to it that on a given evening Mr De Selby is not at home. I think I can arrange that without much trouble. When he is out, there will be nobody else there. And our intrusion will be brief.

– Succinctly so, by dad.

– When we've got the container we will hide it in the shrubbery, near the little gate at the Vico Road. We will then go home. The following morning early I will collect it in a taxi. Then leave the rest to me. The only little snag is how to get into the house.

– That would not be a fastidious worry, the sergeant replied pleasantly, for if he is as careless as you say, I could deal deftly with a window, without wincing.

– But not break one, I hope. We don't want to alarm or alert him.

93

– No then. I have a good pen-knife.

– Ah, that is the business, Sergeant. We can take it that everything is agreed then?

– Except the date of the accomplishment.

– Yes. I'll let you know that in good time.

Mick rose, and in good conspirator's fashion, put out his hand. The sergeant grasped it.

– To the grand defence and preservation of the race of Adam, he intoned solemnly.

10

For Mick a short time of inactivity and rest was to follow, and he was glad of it. He now had a plan to meet this D.M.P. menace and felt that hasty or impetuous moves would do nothing but harm. It was his own plan, with himself as the only real performer, the other two – Hackett and Sergeant Fottrell – being unsuspecting associates. He thought it was wise to avoid meeting either for the time being, for top secrecy was essential; questions by either – particularly the inquisitive Hackett – could lead only to embarrassing evasions.

Mary had not returned and possibly would not before his meeting with Father Cobble, to be followed by a call the same evening on De Selby. That was the next move in the natural sequence, and nothing could be done to accelerate it. What could a week matter in this sombre situation? It seemed to be in character to be leisurely himself in the diabolical scheme he had outlined. Mick's curiosity about how he aimed to distribute his lethal chemical simultaneously all over the world had much abated, for if his own simple plan worked, the interest of the question was academic.

Thus for some days his life was quiet, almost decorous. He thought a bit about his growing, if secret, importance in the world he walked, his quiet command of the issues in a confrontation that was quite fabulous. And what little weapon fortified the iron calm of his nerves? The answer to that, he was sure, was Vichy water.

His attendance at his small job was perhaps more perfunctory than usual; in the evening he usually went for a swim at nearby Blackrock, had a few minerals afterwards, then home and early to bed. He kept feeling, not without pride, that he was taking the correct, easy-going, civilized course of De Selby himself in face of portentous possibility and unheard-of katabolism.

However, one day at lunch-time he made a small, subordinate move. It was within the plan but he went about it with what may be called casual care. His general lack of domestic responsibility, his easy day-to-day spending of everything he earned and his rather improvident attitude to existence were all possible reasons why he never had a bank account and was quite inexperienced in the rubric of writing cheques. Now he gathered together small sums he had put aside at home, sold some books and a pocket watch he never used and did not need and found he had £25, and a little over. He went to the head office of the Bank of Ireland at College Green in the centre of Dublin and, after seeing some important official, opened a current account with a lodgment of £21, and received his first cheque-book. Very silly, of course, but he could not suppress a small surge of elation. Yet there had been no question of bolstering up his personal dignity: there had been another, a solid reason.

The first day of September was a Saturday. On the preceding evening some uneasiness came upon him. It would be necessary to see Hackett soon to instruct him in his role. Since Mick would be in Dalkey on Saturday evening anyway, there seemed to be no objection to making a trip to

95

the Colza on Friday on chance of meeting him and spying out the land generally. It was not unlikely but he might get some tidings of De Selby also.

He pondered the matter, then told himself to stop being punctilious and self-conscious about trivialities, and took a tram to Dalkey about nine in the evening.

The Colza Hotel was quiet and indeed from the outside looked deserted but in the Slum department of the bar he found Dr Crewett and young Nemo Crabbe conversing civilly, with Mrs Laverty behind the counter, knitting. He saluted everybody, ordered a Vichy water and sat down.

– Well, gentlemen, he asked, has there been any sign of my friend Hackett?

Dr Crewett nodded.

– Yes, he said. The gentleman was in earlier with that precocious lady of his. I think he is teaching her to swim.

– We didn't like to ask outright, Crabbe said, because that friend of yours has an uncertain temper, particularly when taking refreshments. He might think we were spying.

Dr Crewett gave a smile which was perhaps more a leer.

– You must remember, Mick, that in teaching a lady to swim, you must first pick out a quiet, inconspicuous part of the shore, and then you must help her to take all her clothes off.

Crabbe guffawed at this.

– She hadn't a whole damn lot to take off, he chuckled.

– Ah it doesn't matter, Mick said easily. I just wanted to mention something to him – nothing important. Any other news, good or bad?

– Nothing much, the doctor said.

– It's a slack time, Mick remarked.

– Wasn't there something about the P.P.? Crabbe interposed.

– There was vague talk about the P.P. being annoyed about something and ordering Sergeant Fottrell to call on him. Probably tales of inadequate bathing costumes down at

White Rock, sunbathing or some other nonsense of the kind. Some prurient busybody trying to make trouble.

— I don't think it was that, doctor, Mick said.

— This is a terrible country for sexual obsession, Crabbe remarked. I give you five cities — Tyre, Sidon, Gomorrah, Sodom and Dublin.

— No. I heard that Teague McGettigan's nag misbehaved himself, in the opinion of his reverence, all around the grounds of the parochial house.

Dr Crewett laughed.

— Mrs Laverty, he called, give us two more drinks here and a Vichy water for my poor friend. Dear me, that's good. 'The Role of the Horse in History'. Paul Revere's Ride; the Charge of the Light Brigade; the Wooden Horse of Troy; and the Catharsis of Teague's Cabhorse.

— I saw the animal only once, Crabbe said, and I'm surprised that he had the energy for such a performance.

They attended to their new drinks.

— Yes, Crabbe added, there's another item of news, very trivial. I got digs, not here but in Dunleary. A woman by the name of Muldowney. A clean enough place. I have hardly anything to eat there except breakfast. Mrs Muldowney hates drink, denounces it strongly and constantly, and takes any God's amount of it.

— On the QT, of course, Mick agreed, thinking of Curley's Tonic Wine.

The conversation had become desultory, tending to lapse. There was simply nothing to talk about.

— It's a pity, Mick ventured at last, that most of us haven't the money to go and live abroad. Our sort of people seem to flourish in an alien clime. One reason may be that this country's too damp.

— It's too full of humbugs and hypocrites, Crabbe said.

— We like to think, Dr Crewett said, that the Irish are the main people who built the modern United States. I think it's true that they and the Italians, both sterling Roman Catholic races, are answerable for the enduring system of crime and vice in America.

Under the skin Dr Crewett was a true misanthrope.

— It was more of the European mainland I was thinking, Mick explained, and, of course, Britain. Shaw would have rotted if he'd stayed here. And look at Stanford, John Field, Tom Moore, Hugh Lane and even Balfe. Consider the wonderful international reputation won by the late James Joyce, most of his life a poor refugee, a miserable fugitive of a teacher in schools all over Europe.

Dr Crewett abruptly put down his glass.

— What do you mean 'the late James Joyce'? Are you serious?

— Serious?

— Yes.

— Of course I'm serious.

— I thought everybody knew that Joyce's death — all those reports in foreign newspapers in the confusion of war — was all my eye.

— You mean that Joyce is still alive?

— Certainly I do.

— Then why didn't he contradict the reports? Such unfounded reports could be actionable.

— Because he put the story out himself.

Mick paused here. The doctor was speaking seriously and, in any event, downright levity was foreign to his cynical nature.

— I find that very hard to believe, Mick said finally.

— Anything of Joyce's that I've read, Crabbe observed, I thought very fine and poetic. His *Portrait of the Artist*, for instance. He's a man I would certainly like to meet. Dr Crewett, if he's still alive, where is he?

Dr Crewett made a vague, head-shaking gesture.

— I never heard the full story, he said. There was some scandal, I believe. I don't know whether it was military, marital or moral. He was ordered out of France by the Germans, that much is certain, and it is obvious he couldn't go anywhere eastward. He may initially have made his way to Spain, or got to England with the help of the French Resistance. Anyhow, he was in England and using another name six months after his alleged death.

– But granted that, it is a considerable time ago now. How do you know he's still alive?

I know a man who was speaking to him a matter of months ago. News of his genuine death could not nowadays be distorted or suppressed.

This made Mick quite excited and, in response, Dr Crewett added:

– But what does it matter? It's his own business and, anyway, he has stopped writing.

– Yes, but where is he?

– Could he be in the United States? Crabbe asked. He would certainly be well treated there, probably be given a chair at one of the universities.

– No, he's not, the doctor replied. I don't think it's any secret that he's still alive, but . . . well . . . his actual where-abouts is a confidential matter. I believe a well-known public man is entitled to privacy if he elects to have it, and par-ticularly if there is some good reason for electing to have it.

This rather affected sort of talk made Mick impatient. Very likely it was intended to tease. If Joyce had left the European mainland and was not in America, he must be in Britain, Ireland or the Isle of Man. The continents of Asia and Africa would be unthinkable habitations for such a man. And the Isle of Man was too small for anybody seeking concealment and anonymity. It seemed clear enough that Dr Crewett knew the location of the hide-out and was possibly engendering self-importance by being difficult about the thing. It was a 'confidential matter' then? That was just tomfoolery as far as the doctor was concerned. His courtly considerations, everybody knew, had never deterred him from butting into the private affairs of other people. Mick thought a direct assault was the proper course.

– Now, Dr Crewett, he said as sternly as he could, I don't think it is reasonable to withhold *any* information about Joyce from the like of me. You know that I greatly esteem the man and that I would be solicitous in any way I could for his well-being. If in fact I knew where he was living – or hiding, if you like – I would absolutely respect his desire to remain unknown and concealed. I would be the last in the world to make such information public property.

The doctor betrayed a slight grimace which he quickly concealed with a gulp from his glass.

– My dear man, he said, you know very well there's no question of my not trusting you. I merely meant that any information I was given was given as being under the rose, strictly confidential. You understand? Ah, we'll talk about it again.

– Very good, Mick said shortly. As you please.

He was sure he knew what the doctor meant: he preferred to say nothing in the presence of Nemo Crabbe, still comparatively a stranger to all of them.

– Crabbe, Mick said brightly, have you managed to become a little more reconciled to the toilsome process of becoming a medical doctor?

Crabbe pulled his mouth into a scowl.

– Not a bit of it, he replied. So far as I can see, we students of today are laboriously studying to obtain a certificate that we're out of date. Revolutionary advances in diagnosis, treatment and pharmacology take place every few months nowadays. A new wonder-drug makes dozens of familiar medicaments obsolete overnight. Look at penicillin and the antibiotics generally.

Yes, that was an intelligent enough point, Mick thought. Would it be appropriate here to expatiate on Sergeant Fottrell's bicyclosis? Hardly.

– When Fleming accidentally produced what he called penicillin in 1928, Dr Crewett observed, he did not invent something or discover anything new. When I was a young fellow in the County Carlow I often saw farm labourers treating boils on the back of their necks by anchoring putrescent cow-dung to the infected place, usually with a dirty scarf. This dung quietly wiped out the staphylococci.

Mick seemed to have some vague recollection of that kind himself.

– Well, Fleming got the Nobel prize, he said. For what?

– What he did was a sheer accident in the lab, the doctor rejoined, but he deserved great credit for accurately observing what he saw, and scientifically recording it.

– But the introduction of penicillin, Mick protested, was a veritable upheaval in the treatment of a great many diseases.

– I've got a good few shots of that stuff in my time, Crabbe said.

– Fleming's secondary achievement, Dr Crewett said, was to synthesize the fungoid process by devising artificial cultures. But the intrinsic secret of penicillin was known to folk medicine for centuries, possibly for thousands of years.

– Yes, I feel that's true.

– That's why it's foolish for men in western Europe to be supercilious about witch-doctors, their brews and decoctions, eye of newt and toe of frog, and so on. Those savages knew nothing of chemistry or pathology but they were capable of carrying on uncomprehended but sound medicinal traditions. The birds and the brute creation have similar instinctive remedies for their own sicknesses.

– Let us have another drop, Mrs Laverty, Crabbe called, and then I must be off about my business.

Mrs Laverty came out from her fortress and arranged the glasses, remarking that it was very close and that she thought there was thunder in the air, judging by her corns, which were at her.

– Leaving aside the stupidities of academic training in medicine, Crabbe said coarsely, who the hell wants to be a G.P.?

– It's a way of life, Dr Crewett said. Even a very bad doctor can earn a living.

– Earn a living, yes, Crabbe returned, but heavens, what a life!

– Better than working in the salt mines.

Crabbe drank with a little tinge of savagery.

– If and when I qualify, he rasped, I'm sure I'll make a damn fool of myself in some unusual way, perhaps like Schweitzer or Livingstone.

– Well then you'll be famous, Dr Crewett replied sardonically, and admired all over the world.

– Aw, go to hell.

Pseudo-technical dialogues of this kind did not interest Mick very much, and he scarcely heard the rest of it. After Crabbe had departed, he turned afresh on Dr Crewett.

– I'm reasonably sure that Joyce is somewhere in this country, for it is inconceivable that he would live in England, and Dublin, congenial as even the changed town of today might be, would be too dangerous for a famous man whose plight was that he must not be recognized. Where is he?

The doctor smiled craftily.

– I told you the information I have is confidential, he declared, which means that if I impart it to you, you must receive it in confidence and in no circumstances pass it on to anybody else.

This was more morbid humbug, Mick concluded, but there was no harm on his part in a naïve play of reciprocation.

– I accept that but subject to one condition. As a piece of information I will keep it to myself. But I would feel entitled to use it merely to make contact with Joyce himself and, on doing that, it is possible he might release me from the obligation of keeping his whereabouts quiet. I might be able to show that his fears, whatever they are, are illusory.

– Oh, I could scarcely question that except that if you did run Joyce to earth, he'd be pretty certain to ask you how you knew where to look for him. I certainly wouldn't like my own name to be mentioned.

– Do you know him?

– No, I don't.

– Then the point is immaterial, though in any case I wouldn't dream of mentioning your name.

Dr Crewett's little passing frown seemed to say that he was not pleased that his existence should thus be summarily discarded.

– Tell me, he said. What do you want to see Joyce about? Why do you want to meet him?

Quite a question, that: gratuitous, impertinent, stupid.

– Anybody's reasons for wishing to know the man should be obvious enough, Mick said coldly. In my own case, the first reason is curiosity. I believe the picture of himself he has conveyed in his writings is fallacious. I believe he must be a far better man or a far worse. I think I have read all his works, though I admit I did not properly persevere with his play-writing. I consider his poetry meretricious and mannered. But I have an admiration for all his other work, for his dexterity and resource in handling language, for his precision, for his subtlety in conveying the image of Dublin and her people, for his accuracy in setting down speech authentically, and for his enormous humour.

As a spontaneous appraisal of literary work, this unpremeditated pronouncement was not bad at all, Mick thought. But after all, was he not a well-read man for his age and upbringing, and fearless enough in facing books in which might lurk danger to morals? He was.

Dr Crewett put down his glass.

– Well by the damn, he said, you are certainly fond of your Joyce. I never suspected you of such enthusiasms.

Mick allowed goodwill to return to his face.

– You might remember that this Colza is not exactly a literary salon. Such matters do not properly arise here as a subject of converse.

– True, I suppose. True.

– I've read some of the stupid books written *about* Joyce

and his work, mostly by Americans. A real book about Joyce, springing from many long talks with him, could clear up misunderstandings and mistakes, and eliminate a lot of stupidity.

– Lord, don't tell me that you are also an author and exegetist in your own right?

– No, I don't claim to be that at all but if I could gather together the material, a friend of mine would be well able to turn it into a fine, fresh book. I happen to know somebody who can write very well. Stylishly.

– Well . . . that's an idea.

– My point is that such a development could take place without disclosing to the public Joyce's present abode.

– I quite see that, but perhaps Joyce wouldn't be so convinced of the prudence of such a publication, with its implication that the master is not dead at all.

Mick finished his drink abruptly.

– I think we've had enough of this skirmishing, Dr Crewett. Where is James Joyce living at the present time?

– In Skerries.

It would be mere shadow of the truth to say that this disclosure deeply startled the enquirer, though it is not easy exactly to say why. Joyce had to be *somewhere*. Skerries is a small, pretty watering-place twenty miles north of Dublin with an ample, sandy strand very safe for youngsters, a spot for deep-sea swimmers on a rocky headland, and round the corner a neat little harbour. Perhaps Mick's surprise that Joyce should be living in such a place grew from the fact that he himself knew it, and liked it well. When a schoolboy he had spent ten days there, and had many times since made a daily trip to revisit the scene. In fact it was there that he had first learned to swim, and it was there he first met Hackett. Was it now an ominous sort of place, a social hazard? Perhaps.

It was surprising, too, that Joyce should go to ground so near Dublin city, in fact in the County Dublin.

Yet what was so funny? Perhaps Skerries was a sagacious

choice. As a resort it had its season – a long season, for it is in an area famous for its very light rainfall. The natives were quite accustomed to having strangers and visitors in their midst, and even retired people who remain on in town out of season. Most householders who had the accommodation took guests. Yes, perhaps here again one had silence, exile and cunning.

– Well, that is very interesting, doctor, Mick said briskly, and certainly unexpected. Have we any other information?

– I don't know his address, if that's what you mean.

– That wouldn't bother me. I'd ferret that out on the spot. Are there any other particulars? For instance, is he using his own name in any situation where he must produce *some* name?

– No. I know absolutely nothing more but wouldn't be surprised to know he's using his own name.

– Ah, well well. Does he drink, for instance, and if so, where? Or would he have a morning cup of coffee in some pretty little shop?

Dr Crewett smiled bleakly.

– No information. I think I've told you everything I know – and that's very little – but I imagine his life would be rather that of a recluse.

Mick pondered his little clues and they seemed to make up quite a workable pattern, considering that only a little seaside town he knew well was the territory.

– Well, thanks very much, doctor, for all the secrets you've given me, and so generously.

– In confidence, mind, he said, wagging his finger waggishly.

It was not long until Mick was making his way to a homeward tram. He was preoccupied. It was strange how fast somewhat grisly spices were accumulating on his platter. First, the central menace of De Selby, and his own plan to foil him. Then the baffling Saint Augustine episode. Next, the accidental Father Cobble complication, to be enacted on the morrow. And now this Joyce phantasm, a man back from beyond the grave, armed only with the plea that he had never gone there, yet hiding under a name unknown in a little town.

Surely it was enough to baffle any man, if not frighten him? Yet Mick was on the edge of congratulating himself that he was the phlegmatic type, one who was not without his own cunning, a gift for scheming, and a certain rough courage.

As the tram lurched on its way, he became certain of one thing. He would go to Skerries, for a matter of days if necessary, search every nook and cranny of it, and find Joyce if he was there. He would strip him of all his secrets, his dreams, boasts and regrets, and present them on a tray to that unpredictable, domineering, able, fascinating girl Mary. Would she thank him, though – or tell him off for meddling in the affairs of strangers? Hardly . . . not surely in the case of a man like Joyce. She had herself advanced no mean distance in the Republic of Letters, knew a lot more about French literature than he did. She was inquisitive concerning the nature of genius, personally creative and therefore receptive. No. The true story of Joyce would be ideal material for the exercise of her rich mind. She would produce her own unprecedented book.

I I

At the time of these events, the Royal Marine Hotel in Dunleary was a big hulk of faded splendour, with hints of red plush and gilt of bygone good times. Yet there was comfort there still, good food, and the peculiar solace which sometimes can be got from cross-channel accents.

Mick arrived twenty minutes too early, sat in the lounge and fortified himself with a precautionary glass of the French water. His intention was to represent to Father Cobble that De Selby was an eccentric man, though of exceptional intellectual powers, and that he seemed spiritually very confused; and that perhaps he would be the better for a straightforward talk on the immutability of the Christian ideal, the immortality of the soul, and the respect which was due to the Church. He aimed also to steer a theme, such as the propagation throughout the world of Christ's message, round to the nature of the secret scheme which De Selby was harbouring for dissemination simultaneously everywhere of his ghastly D.M.P. He saw it would be worse than futile to inform Father Cobble about the unearthly problem which confronted him in his effort to shield mankind from an unparalleled sort of threat.

Father Cobble came punctually. He had the look which his deep booming voice had told Mick he would have – a thin, dark, very small man of sixty or so, with a lined but pleasant, well-meaning face. He was very well-dressed. As he paused in the large lounge gazing enquiringly about him, Mick rose, went to his side, touched his arm and put his hand out.

– Father Cobble, I think?

– Ah!

He shook hands affably.

– Well, well. You are Michael, of course. Excellent. Capital.

– Perhaps we might sit over here, Father, Mick said, leading the way to his little table. The priest smiled and sat down, neatly stowing his hat and furled umbrella at a nearby stand.

– And isn't it the heavy evening, he said agreeably. I can't say I enjoy this sort of heat. I've spent many years in Rome; the thermometer's higher, there, of course, but somehow it's a different sort of heat.

– Everybody says the exhausting thing here is the humidity

of the atmosphere, Father, but I've never quite understood what that means.

Father Cobble was looking brightly about him.

– I think we may take it that the strong sunlight of summer extracts vapours from our sodden landscape, he remarked, but I imagine that situation is beyond human redress. Of course in some big cities, particularly in America, the problem is met indoors by air conditioning. Our own house in Cleveland has this arrangement and, believe me, it makes an enormous difference. Well now! What about a nice cup of tea and perhaps some sugartops?

– *Sugartops*?

– Yes, yes. You know, those little circular cakes with icing on top, white or pink. I'm serious.

What a horrible suggestion! Was this sybaritism as understood by the Jesuits? Mick gave what was intended to sound like a gentle little laugh.

– Father, I couldn't possibly.

– Ah, perhaps tea then with freshly-cut ham sandwiches?

– You see, Father, I usually do not have a proper lunch in the middle of the day. This means that I am a ravening wolf when I get home in the evening, and then I plough into a great dinner. It is not an hour since I laid down my knife and fork.

Father Cobble chuckled and surprisingly produced a packet of cigarettes.

– Let me confess the truth, he said. I am in the same boat. Do have a cigarette. We also dine in the evening. I'm afraid our House has brought some exotic customs here.

– No harm. The Irish Church is very insular. He pointed to his glass, not yet quite empty. If I might make a suggestion, Father, I think both of us deserve a drop of decent drink. A curiosity is that whiskey is an antidote to heat. When empire-builders have to live in hot foreign climates abroad, they consume great quantities of whiskey. At the moment I happen to be ignoring whiskey for a secret little reason of my own but I insist that you have a glass of Kilbeggan.

– Well now, perhaps that is an idea, Michael.

Mick ignored his detestable familiarity, beckoned a waiter and ordered the two drinks. Father Cobble was now smoking, relaxed, and gazing with interest about him.

– Well now. You have a friend who is in trouble?

– Not exactly in trouble, Father. At least I think he would be astonished if anybody told him he was, and offered sympathy. It is only that some of his attitudes and ways of thinking have struck me as eccentric, not to say unbalanced.

– Yes. Would I be right in saying that strong drink is involved here?

This reading amused Mick a little. What could be simpler than alcoholism, a spirituous rather than a spiritual disorder? He would be very happy indeed if that was all the trouble with De Selby.

– Oh not at all, Father. He is by no means a strict T.T. any more than you or I, but I would define the origin of his trouble as an overweening intellectual arrogance.

– Ah. The old sin of pride.

– His name is De Selby and he is a sort of a scientist.

– A foreigner caught up with some pagan dialectic?

– He is not a foreigner. He speaks exactly like a Dublin man, and the word 'pagan' would not occur to me in connexion with him. In fact he believes in God and claims to have verified the divine existence by experiment. I think you could say he lacks the faith because he is in no need of it. He *knows.*

He could sense Father Cobble turning his head slightly and staring.

– What an extraordinary man, he said. Yes. We priests in the line of duty do come across a great number of very strange people. One must be careful. If drink be not in question, how can you be sure there is no narcosis of some other kind?

– One cannot be certain of anything like that, of course,

Mick replied, but he is absolutely rational, occasionally even brilliant, in his talk. You can judge for yourself shortly.

– Indeed yes. May I ask – this is mere polite curiosity – why you thought I could be of help?

– To be honest, I didn't. That was somebody else's idea. But I'm sure a man of your attainments, Father, could not fail to do good in any situation. And you will be relieved to hear that De Selby is invariably polite, urbane and civilized. I suspect, indeed, that he enjoys argument. And he is an authority on the Bible.

He could see that Father Cobble's attitude and appetite were being whetted. He was glad of this, because theological conversational infighting between him and De Selby might put the latter off his guard so far as he, Mick, was concerned and he thus might somehow leak his scheme for the simultaneous worldwide deployment of D.M.P. But this, he had to remind himself, lacked the importance it initially had, for if his own plan were successfully put into operation and in time, De Selby with all his works and pomps would be a nullity, at least for the time being.

Father Cobble had very smartly finished his glass of malt, summoned a waiter and ordered similar drinks, which he paid for with a ten shilling note. Mick was a bit surprised. The internal mechanics of the Jesuit Order (or Society, as they called themselves) was to him a mystery. It was one of the mendicant orders but he thought this term had a technical meaning. How could mendicants live in the grandiose palaces and colleges which the Jesuits customarily inhabit? The answer seemed to be that every Jesuit Father – and postulant for that matter – is personally a mendicant inasmuch as he is forbidden to have any means or goods whatsoever. If his duties call for him to make a journey, across the town or across the world, he has to go to some superior or bursar and ask for his fare. It appeared that the Order was very wealthy, its members utterly indigent. He had heard that the Fathers lived and ate well in their princely abodes. Good luck to them!

On the short tram journey to Dalkey they went upstairs, for Father Cobble was still engaged very earnestly with a cigarette. Mick was wondering whether smoking was forbidden *intra muros* and was the priest, in a sort of a way, mitching? But he did not like to ask. Indeed, as a non-smoker himself, it was none of his business. The subject of their conversation was, curiously, swimming. Father thought it was an excellent exercise, taught discipline and self-reliance, and one never knew when this skill would come in useful, even to the point of saving life. No, he could not swim himself. It had been his life-long regret that his student days had been spent in inland establishments without even a decent river at hand. The country was backward insofar as providing swimming-baths for schools and colleges was concerned. Certain tasks and habits should be inculcated in early youth, the formative time of life. A priest friend of his, a keen swimmer, had told him of an amusing experience at the Forty Foot at Sandycove. His reverence was in the water when a very fat man arrived, undressed very quickly, accidentally bashed a toe on a sharp dagger of rock on his way to the water, fell and severely gashed his elbow. He sat there, cursing and bellowing forth the most lurid language, but his face quickly changed colour when the man in the water emerged to towel himself and then don the clothes of a priest, collar and all. Father Cobble laughed softly at his own story. Clearly he was a man of the world. Had the two glasses of whiskey slackened the grip of austerity which, Mick reflected, is not natural or permanent with any man.

Their walk up the Vico Road was pleasant and tranquil, and the seaward prospect as enchanting as ever in the softness of the evening. But finally there they were, a little after eight, standing outside De Selby's door.

He opened it himself, playing out immediately his undeniable charm, relieved his visitors of hats and umbrella and led the way into the room in which Hackett and Mick had first conferred with him. De Selby was clearly in good spirits and Mick hoped vaguely that this was not occasioned by a new break-through in the diabolical laboratory.

– I may tell you, Father Cobble, he said, and you, Michael, that I've done something which may seem rude but not so intended. I have ordered Teague McGettigan to call with his cab at ten o'clock to drive you to the tram. Do you know, it can be cold these nights when the sun goes down.

They expostulated cheerfully about this arrangement, of course, but it pleased Father Cobble, who discerned it to be a friendly gesture. Then the talk began, only to be interrupted temporarily while De Selby produced his home-made whiskey, this time in a large decanter – glasses and water. It seemed that he had correctly divined Father Cobble's taste in this thing. Mick instinctively knew that this was no time to start a dialogue about Vichy water, something new in his relations with De Selby. Duty bade him silently acquiesce in whiskey, even if it choked him.

Talk was rather desultory, partly due to De Selby's politeness as host, partly because Father Cobble, an Englishman, was also polite and academic and seemed to lack polemical ardour or to have real appetite for argument. Mick felt he had to start something or somehow attend to the management of this meeting, if the occasion was not to be inarticulate futility. He patiently waited for the lull which would enable him to cast his fly.

– Father Cobble, our host Mr De Selby has perfected a chemical organism – I do not understand exactly what it is – which, he considers, would be of inexpressible benefit to communities of men throughout the world. If I understand the situation aright, his problem is to make this substance available universally at the same time, as an atmospheric change in one place could cause havoc in another unless a comparable change could have been synchronistically arranged for the other . . .

– Dear me, Father Cobble murmured.

– Please continue, De Selby said benignly. It is always valuable to hear another person define what he is pleased to call one's problems.

Mick blushed faintly but was unshaken in his aim to induce De Selby to say something to Father Cobble about D.M.P.

– Well, he continued, this idea of mine is probably outlandish but I thought there might be some parallel between the propagation of the faith and the worldwide dissemination of this substance.

– Good gracious now, Father Cobble said, evidently stimulated, setting down his glass. That is certainly an interesting query, outlandish or not. It is rather as if a large manufacturer of tobacco were to include in his packet a slip telling the smoker which were the best matches to use.

De Selby had lit a cigarette, not having offered one to the priest: this seemed a personal quirk of his.

– There is really no problem, Father, he said.

– But this is interesting. In the present state of the world, missionary work has taken on a totally new character. This globe of ours has shrunk pathetically. Modern achievements in radio and television, tape recording and all the magic of the cinema have so radically improved communication – *communication*, I repeat – that the old-fashioned preacher going into the wilds is now almost obsolete. Beside the pulpit we may now place the microphone. I mean, Mr De Selby, that these organs of communication are equally open to yourself.

This was not the way Mick wanted the subject to be handled.

– Gentlemen, he said, I've already said that my suggestion was outlandish. I don't think really that there is any parallel because, while the Church is disseminating an idea, a faith, Mr De Selby's task is disseminating a thing, a commodity. There is a big difference. An idea could be infectious, sweep-

ing pell-mell over an entire community. But not so a thing.
– What exactly is this substance or commodity? Father
Cobble asked, puzzled.
– I believe it changes the air, Mick replied.
– Let us say it is an atmospheric rejuvenator, De Selby said,
perhaps not unlike, in its effects, the apparatus they have in
big cinemas for changing the air every two minutes.
– Would it be suitable for use in large churches?
– Well, I hadn't thought of that.

It was clear that Father Cobble's interest was not casual.
It may be that he had had training as a physicist and was
accustomed to speculation about the purely mechanistical lot
of man on this earth. He said that if it was shown beyond all
doubt that 'this invention' was good and of true benefit to
the human race, the Church would certainly not oppose it.
But whether the great ecclesiastical organizations could be
properly called in to encourage its adoption and use – that
was another question. The Church was ever watchful where
strictly lay matters were sought to be obtruded within its
sacred jurisdiction. He recollected that when it was first proposed that concrete should be used in the construction of
churches, there was quite a to-do, and the matter had to be
referred to Rome. Missionaries brought not only the faith to
unenlightened peoples but also most of the boons of modern
hygiene – clean drinking water, baths, lavatories, insecticides
and all manner of medicaments to counter the depredations
of mice, monkeys, rats, beetles and cockroaches. *Mens sana
in corpore sano* was indeed a very wise adage. The air in
many parts of the pagan world – particularly in Africa – was
far from satisfactory or salubrious. The climate was the root
of the trouble. In parts of Africa the air was fetid, and
charged with a deplorable stench. Did Mr De Selby think his
preparation could retrieve such a situation?

De Selby replied that he hesitated to go so far. In reality
his little atmospheric preoccupation was still at the stage of
experiment. His main interest in the air we breathe was its

gaseous constitution. Was its nitrogenous content ideal, for instance?

It was plain enough to Mick that the wily old sage was lying, if one allows that there was any real meaning in his talk at all. He had no intention of divulging the truth about D.M.P.

Father Cobble said it was most advisable that so important and useful an intervention in the physical world should be brought to adjudication as soon as possible; men gifted with large ideas of that kind had a duty before God to develop them.

De Selby said that he was under certain difficulties. This was not a matter that could be investigated by a vast pharmaceutical laboratory. It entailed research, so far as he was concerned, and several departments of this new science were inchoate and obscure. Probably no physicist would be qualified to join him in his studies. This was not to say he was held up by mere shortage of staff. Far from it. His experiments were almost at an end. He was now at the stage of checking and verifying various conclusions which had emerged from his work over many years. It had been hard endeavour but the end-product, so to speak, was in sight.

He then courteously shared out more drink.

His own Society, Father Cobble pointed out, was not properly ranked among the missionary orders. Theirs was the task of disciplining the Church's roster for intellectual duty. It was a heavy burden but they were willing indeed to assume it and he thought he could proudly say that they were making a job of it! Two ideas occurred to him. There were several renowned Jesuit universities in the world and it was more than possible that the department of physics in one of them could be of valuable assistance to Mr De Selby. Some of the most distinguished men in that sphere were members of the Society. The second idea concerned a brother of his own. His brother had sound scientific training and had always had that valuable stimulus – curiosity. True, he was at present head of a small boot polish factory at Leeds, but it might be remembered that he was a B.Sc. of Glasgow University. Father Cobble thought this scientist would be happy to come over for a chat with Mr De Selby.

The latter was grateful for the offer but, really, such a visit would be an imposition on the decent man. Research, properly so-called, was at an end. Nothing remained but the tying of loose ends.

Mick, in a final return to the attack, pointed out to De Selby that the question he had originally raised was not the intrinsic merit of the product or its impact on mankind but its simultaneous dispersal throughout the world.

De Selby laughed.

– Faith now but you seem obsessed with difficulties, even when they're not there. What's wrong with the Post Office?

– The *Post Office*?

– Certainly. If I wanted to send letters out to arrive simultaneously in London and New York, nothing is necessary beyond a brief glance at postal times. If I had a thousand packages to despatch so that all would arrive on the same day at a different points throughout the globe, I believe a good postman would draw up a schedule of posting times and stamp charges in his spare time for a few guineas.

So that was the plan! Why had it not occurred to Mick, to Hackett, to everybody? Why had they been so obtuse?

It would be a waste of time to enquire to whom the packages would be addressed. It didn't matter: they would be opened anyway – *if* they were ever posted.

Evidently Father Cobble's curiosity had waned somewhat, as his humour grew rosier with De Selby's cheerful distillate.

– The Post Office, he said, is nearly as universal as the Church. I have often thought of that. You walk along a poor, deserted lane. Behold, you see a little letter-box, a post-box, built into the wall. It is perhaps 10,000 miles from Hong

Kong but if you push a letter into it, addressed to Hong Kong, it will miraculously go.

– I agree, Father, Mick said. It's marvellous.

De Selby withdrew to return with a basket of assorted biscuits and to take a fresh, determined grip of the decanter. And that is how the evening went. Shortly after ten a shambling bout of knocking told them that Teague McGettigan had arrived, and Father Cobble and Mick were intoxicated and tired enough to be grateful for this small mercy. De Selby they left, cheerful but unperturbed.

How did Mick feel going homeward with his reverence? Not vexed, not stultified: his own word would be *intact*. He had learnt something, but his plan of campaign was unaffected. Father Cobble was a nonentity. The evening had been pleasant enough but if anybody came out of the encounter with a sad lack of any credit, it was poor Mary.

12

The floor of that apartment in Mick's head which he liked to call the spare room was becoming a bit littered and untidy. Several tides seemed to be running simultaneously on the same shore, if that metaphor serves better. Matters had altered somewhat and he felt that he should now set out, in due order, the problems as they had grown and hardened in his mind, think out in what sequence they should be tackled and the results reconciled. Beforehand let it be agreed that the Father Cobble episode, silly and pointless as it was in the event, had cleared away worry about De Selby's plan for disseminating his poison. Use of the Post Office was true anticlimax, considering the grandeur of the threat, but it removed the question completely from the list of things to be done by Mick, and was also salutary in reminding him that a mind portentous in ingenuity had withal its pathetic simplicities. Here then is the list, as he mentally drew it up, of the imponderable tasks which seemed to confront him.

1. De Selby's cask had to be stolen as soon as possible, with the co-operation of Sergeant Fottrell.

2. To the end of (1) he would make a bogus appointment with De Selby at the Colza Hotel and, by pre-arrangement with Hackett, have him detained there while he, Mick, and the sergeant rifled his house.

3. To the end of (2) he would have to fix on a date, with a time about 9 p.m., and in the meantime see Hackett, taking care to remember to keep Sergeant Fottrell informed.

4. He would have to devise, at a longer remove, a method of ensuring that De Selby would not resume manufacture or production of his deadly D.M.P., for an interim solution of the awful menace was no solution at all. At the same time his Christian conscience forbade the simple killing of De Selby.

5. Investigation of the James Joyce situation at Skerries was an urgent necessity to the greater honour and promotion to celebrity of his virgin Mary, but did he love Mary so fully and deeply as he had been persuading himself he did? Did she secretly despise him?

6. Assuming he met Joyce and won his confidence, could the contretemps at (4) be resolved by bringing together De Selby and Joyce and inducing both to devote their considerable brains in consultation to some recondite, involuted and incomprehensible literary project, ending in publication of a book which would be commonly ignored and thus be no menace to universal sanity? Would Joyce take to De Selby, and vice versa? Does a madman reciprocally accept a dissimiliar madness? Could the conjunction of the two conceivably bring forth something more awful even than D.M.P.? (All those were surely very harassing puzzles.)

7. Was he losing sight of the increase and significance of his own personal majesty? Well, it seemed that he had been, probably out of the force of habit of his lowly way of life theretofore. Nobody, possibly not even Mary, seemed to think that he mattered very much. But his present situation was that he was on the point of rescuing everybody from obliteration, somewhat as it was claimed that Jesus had redeemed all mankind. Was he not himself a god-figure of some sort?

8. Did not the Saint Augustine apparition mean that all was not well in heaven? Had there been some sublime slip-up? If he now carried out successfully his plan to rescue all God's creatures, was there not a sort of concomitant obligation on him to try at least to save the Almighty as well as his terrestrial brood from all his corrupt Churches – Catholic, Greek, Mohammedan, Buddhist, Hindu and the innumerable manifestations of the witch doctorate?

9. Was it his long-term duty to overturn the whole Jesuit Order, with all its clowns of the like of Father Cobble, or persuade the Holy Father to overturn it once again – or was it his duty to overturn the Holy Father himself?

Those were the sort of questions, or speculations, which filled Mick's mind for some days and nights. They made his head feel like a hive full of bees and he had to remind himself that his own reason must be kept on tight rein. He finally decided that the De Selby D.M.P. transaction was paramount, as most of the others largely depended on it. Depending on a chance encounter with Hackett in Dalkey was awkward and time-wasting and the first step was to make an appointment with him (which he forthwith did by postcard) to meet at 6 p.m. after work two evenings later in the bar of Westland Row railway station in Dublin city. Such a location may seem odd and conspiratorial but nothing of that kind was intended: it was a quiet, free-and-easy place, little known to passing citizens, and perhaps his choice of it was prompted by so simple a thing as that it gave both of them a convenient way of getting home afterwards by rail. That at least was the sort of triviality that seemed to keep obtruding on his grandiose affairs.

He kept that appointment and Hackett arrived, as usual, late. And he was not in his pleasantest mood. He followed a rather coarse greeting with a complaint.

– If you want to see me about something, that's fair enough, but on a hot dry evening like this when what I want is a pint, why must you fix on a place where they don't serve pints?

Mick decided to be unresponsive and precise, since his business was important.

– All we have to do, he replied, is walk down the stairs to the street and into any nearby pub. Alternatively we can stay here and you can have a whiskey as a consolation, or even a large coffee. I'm drinking Vichy water for a change, for the good of my guts, and it's not everywhere you get it. They have it here.

– What's wrong with the Colza?

– It's too far away.

– All right. Get me a whiskey.

They sat down at the back and Mick tried to explain his needs concisely. He wanted to raid De Selby's house to get something and he would invent some colourable pretext for meeting him at the Colza Hotel. He would not be there but it would be Hackett's job to hold De Selby there in conversation and if possible ply him with drinks. The question was – which evening?

– What do you want to rob the poor bastard of? That barrel of chemicals he has?

– Perhaps. What does it matter to you?

– Well, Mick, if *you* don't trust De Selby, maybe I don't trust *you*. What are you going to do with the stuff?

– Nothing. That is to say, I intend to leave it in an absolutely safe place, where nobody can get at it and indeed where nobody will know what it is.

Hackett nodded thoughtfully.

– The position seems to be, he said, that De Selby can destroy the world with it. Your proposition is that De Selby's power should be transferred to yourself.

– That is not true, Mick answered very firmly. I do not possess the secret of the stuff's detonation. Only De Selby himself knows that.

– That may be only a half-truth. He may have the formula written down and you might be able to lift that from his desk as well as make off with the barrel.

– Well, by the damn! Is that likely with a man like De Selby?

– It's at least possible.

– My sole purpose is to get this dangerous stuff out of the way for good.

Here Hackett called for another drink.

– Suppose you get only the cask. That's three-quarters of the battle, isn't it? In a situation so critical, what is to prevent you kidnapping De Selby and torturing him until he yields his secrets?

Mick gave a laugh that was genuine enough.

– Hackett, he replied, you're getting fanciful and macabre. It's only in books and on films that things are done that way.

Hackett attended to his glass reflectively.

– Well, he announced finally, I don't give a damn about this thing. If you know what you're doing, it's all right with me. I'm not at all sure what De Selby is really up to, and I don't give a damn if that house of his in the trees is a knocking-shop. Provided De Selby turns up at the Colza I'll keep him there all right and as regards drink, I'll do my best to make him ply *me* with it. You needn't be afraid he'll walk in on you when you've broken into his house. As a matter of fact I'll slip him a Mickey Finn if necessary.

– No, no, that shouldn't be necessary. In fact it would be very undesirable, as we don't want to startle or alarm him.

– Well, I'll bring a dose along just in case.

Here again Mick wanted to be exact.

— My own operation, he explained, won't take long at all. De Selby will naturally find out in due course that his stuff is gone, but what can he do? What would be the point of reporting the theft to the police? I mean, what could he report as having been taken?

— Hurry up and buy another round. He could report the theft of his metal cask. He could say, if he liked, that it was full of gold sovereigns or something else very valuable of the kind.

Mick shook his head.

— Details of a theft must be genuine and particularized, he replied, but what you say reminds me of a possible snag. I don't know the weight of that container. Perhaps it may be too heavy to carry and that my attempt may have to be abandoned for the time being. If things turn out that way, it's all the more reason why you should treat De Selby gently at the Colza. I will leave no marks of forcible entry at his house and he need have no suspicions aroused. That will make way for a second attempt if need be.

He raised his voice.

— Miss, please bring us two drinks of the same.

Hackett seemed satisfied enough.

— Well, all right, he said. But what date? I'm a bit tied up just now. I'm in that inter-pub snooker tournament again. This night week would be the earliest I'd be certain of.

That was a bit late, Mick thought, but argument with Hackett was usually of no avail. The reason he had given to cover a whole week was obviously not genuine. He must have some private gambit of his own on hand. Still, that date would have to serve, for Mick had to make a dud appointment with De Selby in the meantime. Yes. And it occurred to him that within that week it might be possible to pay at least an exploratory visit to Skerries. If he could realize the Joyce contact, he could perhaps arrange the preliminaries of his admittedly rather fanciful nexus between Joyce and De Selby not only for their current good but for the good of all mankind. There seemed to be a prospect that his own activities might knot up together. Life is better simple, he reflected. He accepted Hackett's night, which happened to be a Friday. He told him he would make the appointment at the Colza with De Selby for 8.30 p.m., and that his short visit to the house would begin not later than nine. He said nothing about Sergeant Fottrell.

As they went down the stairs to the street (as he might have known they would instead of getting a train) Hackett asked him whether he would like to join him in a visit to Mulligan's, wherever that was. No, he hadn't a snooker match there in his tournament but he had planned a few games for practice. A great difficulty in this kind of thing, he explained, was the variation in quality of tables and other gear as between pub and pub. Some of the houses didn't seem to know that the cues should be straight, and tipped.

Mick declined the invitation. Though he understood billiards and snooker, he did not play and had always found both games boring as a spectacle – the more skilfully played, the more boring. When they parted he made for the General Post Office and sent this message to Sergeant Fottrell on a letter-card:

Will call next Friday evening at 8.45 to have a stroll and talk about the bicycle race.

Enigmatic, maybe, but unmistakable to the redoubtable Sergeant. He then walked out and sank into one of the public seats at the Nelson Pillar. Two new little questions had come into his head for leisurely adjudication.

Assuming everything went as planned at the Vico Road, he should be free about half nine. Should he then go into the Colza Hotel, with or without the sergeant, and apologize to De Selby for being late for his appointment with him there – yet to be made? He met this query by lazily putting off the decision until the night in question.

Number two – should he in fact use one or even two of the

intervening days to visit Skerries? The answer here was quite clear – *yes* – and it exhilarated him. It was a new direction, a development in his tortuous affairs. There was a sort of challenge there: challenges were to be met, not frowningly put away to be considered another time.

He got up and walked slowly back to Westland Row station. He could get a train home there, of course, but his main purpose was to look up the timetables of the other line, the Great Northern Railway, which served Skerries.

Well, things seemed to be moving at last, he murmured to himself as he got into his home-bound train and the train, as if in agreement, moved out.

13

He examined it idly as it lay on his knee. It looked spent, he thought – perhaps a bit wrinkled for its age and showing signs of wear. Yet it had seen very little real wear. Was it, like a man's face, a reflex of the travail and struggles of the mind? That was possible. He was looking at the back of his right hand as the train rushed through the bright countryside, Dublin's market garden, provenance of new potatoes, peas, beans, strawberries, tomatoes and even mushrooms. It was God's own little pantry, plenteous kingdom of black earth and small rain, always urgent in a flourish of growth and ripening, or generous harvesting. It seemed much more alive than his hand, but maybe there was some melancholy in his mood. There often was, he felt, and reason for it.

The town of Skerries has been referred to on another page but it is not easy to convey the air and style of the place. It was a pleasant, small resort with great variety of sea and shore, broad streets in which lurked a surprising number of thatched houses. The long curved harbour with its border of dwellings, shops and pubs was diminutive and pretty except at low tide when the ebb had left a mess in the basin, mostly of rock, weed and slime. High above, near the railway station, an old windmill kept watch on the quiet people.

He left the train and walked the familiar road downhill. He passed the junction with Church Street, a quiet living quarter, and went on to Strand Street, which is the fine, broad, main thoroughfare of the town. There were plenty of people about – the holiday-makers, resident or visiting, easily to be distinguished. But he kept his own mind in restraint. His mission was investigation, and it seemed that pubs and tea-shops were places to be looked at, though neither fitted in with his mind's picture of James Joyce's nature and habits.

He first tried a tea-shop. What was on offer varied between ice cream, tepid tea and fish-and-chips. He found such surroundings dismal indeed, noticed nobody in the least resembling Joyce and could not believe that the latter's austere and fastidious mind could tolerate such confrontations after the sophisticated *auberges* of Paris or Zürich. The conversation?

– Will you for God's sake stop scratching yourself and drink your lemonade!

– I wonder where that poor bastard Charlie got to after last night's argument?

Then a pub: he soon saw that in general they were the old-fashioned kind, still to be found in small Irish towns – dark, with wooden partitions abutting from the counter at intervals, havens of secrecy and segregation. Of all of them that he visited, carefully restricting his drink to small pale sherries in the interest of vigilance, it is fair to say that they were rather dirty, and nearly always the man behind the bar – whether the boss himself or a curate – was in his shirt-sleeves, and the shirt itself was rarely of the best.

The prospect was discouraging. It was possible, he supposed, that Joyce temporarily took refuge somewhere else to escape the descent of witless holiday crowds during the summer. The exile, refugee or runaway has no roots, even in his own country.

One house looked a bit secluded and reserved, and he entered. Yes, it was dark, with a few small knots of men gathered about their dark drinks. The man of the house was a squat, round-faced jovial person of sixty-five, attired to counter-height in a stained pullover. Mick saluted as gaily as he could and asked for a small sherry. This was presented affably enough.

– You look to me like another Dublin man, me good sir, he beamed. The crowd that thinks they keep Skerries alive.

– Well, I'm from that direction, Mick admitted civilly.

– Begob then and good luck to what they have in their trousers pockets. Know what they keep there?

– A few bob, I suppose.

– They keep their hands there.

– Is trade bad, then?

– Ah, not at all, I wouldn't say that. But it's our own crowd and a wild crowd that comes here from Balbriggan and Rush that keeps this old town on its feet. All that holiday scruff isn't worth a damn, when they get two bottles down or maybe three, they think they're gone to the limit of deeboocherie. And bottles of what, though?

– Well, stout, I suppose. Not whiskey, surely?

– Phwaugh! Bottles of Dootch lagger. I have to lay it in specially in the summer. And do you know what it is? It's piss, that's what it is. Horse's piss.

– How do you know what horse's piss tastes like? Mick asked, pleased with the question.

– How . . . how do I know? I had a few pints of it meself in Dublin a few years ago. You'd smell the Clydesdale off of it.

Mick drank politely, and smiled. The natural garrulity of publicans could be a real help in his quest.

– Ah well, he said, every man to his own poison, I suppose. Matter of fact, I ran down here only for a day or two. I heard a rumour that there's an uncle of mine living about here somewhere, calls himself Captain Joyce, I believe. Lost touch with him a good few years ago. A slightly built man with glasses, elderly.

The publican seemed to shake his head.

– Joyce? No, I don't think so. There's so many people coming and going here, you know. Does he take e'r a smahan of Jameson or Tullamore?

– I'm not sure. I know he was abroad. Perhaps he'd be more inclined to have a drop of wine, or maybe a liqueur.

– *Wine?*

The very word seemed to be startling.

– Ah no, not at all, not here. I never had that class of person on the premises, though there's one old army gentleman here that drinks port till the stuff comes out in his socks. But his name is Stewart.

– Oh, it doesn't matter. I suppose I'll ask a few other people but it's really only curiosity. My real purpose is to get some of that salty fresh air you have down here.

– Well, no shortage of that, and no charge for it.

Mick finished his drink and went out. Where else to go? The next nearest pub, of course.

The result there was negative. The shop was low-roofed, gloomy, and the uncommunicative man behind the counter seemed to have the grey bloom of disease on his face. Mick had another small sherry.

– How's the season going this year? he enquired of a non-descript bystander.

– Good few here, the latter replied, and one of them's meself.

That much was already proclaimed by open-necked shirt and his short drink, which was not whiskey: probably brandy.

– Well, Mick said, it's a good place for a quiet rest.

– Could be but not when you have to bring the whole
bloody family along. The kids, the wife *and* the wife's sister.

No use, this. Saying 'Anything's better than being on your
own', Mick went out. This seemed a very hole-and-corner
procedure. It was now half-five, too early in the evening for
the public houses to show their full strength. The air was
sultry, with little sun. He remembered the contents of the
small parcel he had brought, just in case: pyjamas, a towel
and bathing togs. He went for a stroll right around the harbour, disdaining the pubs there, got to the headland and
walked on till he found a seat near the swimming place
known as the Captain's, available at all levels of tidewater.
He rested there, digesting his frugal drink and lazily viewing
the great semi-circular white-yellow strand below, with
groups of people resting with children, dressing or un-
dressing or trying to read. It was a scene of disengagement
and repose, the common belief being that an interval of this
sort of thing at least once a year was very good for one. Yet
he always recoiled from formal summer holidays in a place
like Skerries. With the money available, he felt the civilized
thing would be a few weeks earlier in the year in the Rhine-
land, Paris, perhaps Rome and the Mediterranean.

Time, a diluted sort of time, drifted past him, and perhaps
he dozed. When he bestirred himself, he went down to the
Captain's, stripped and dived in. The incoming tide was
fresh and cool, very pleasant. He felt quite reconditioned
when he afterwards made his way to the hotel dining-room
and asked the waitress to bring him two lightly-boiled fresh
eggs. What he might now call habit made him inspect everybody in this cheerful apartment but no – of Joyce there was
no sign at all. A good few well-got-up people were eating
there, some of them trippers, and a group of loud-voiced
men whom he dismissed as harmless drunks. He remained on
for a while, reading an evening paper and on his way out
paused in the hall to ask the young lady whether she could
give him a bed for the night.

– For one night?

– Yes, but I'm not yet certain I'll need it. I won't know for another few hours or so.

– I'll do my best but it would be safer to book now.

He said he would take a chance and probably look in again later. He had in fact two days' leave to have the chance to follow up any Joyce clue. He had got into the habit of thinking ahead.

Up to then his total calls had numbered five, none of them worth a return. But plenty of public houses remained to be checked over. The feeling of fullness after a meal weakened his earlier resolve about mild sherry but he sternly re-asserted the regimen. He was engaged on work, and important work. There must be no slipping.

It was after seven when he entered a rather poky establishment on the periphery of the harbour. One drink and the use of eye and ear told him there was nothing there. There was a big enough assembly, mostly of strangers, but they were loud and rowdy, and well on the high-road to a late night. No quiet, sardonic novelist loitered there. Yet was there any unhurried nook deemed seemly for a writer's presence? Or was Joyce a recluse tucked away in chimney corner, avoiding all occasions of public concourse, fearing and despising the people and keeping to himself? Mick's own plans apart, he hoped not. A delicate reason could easily become unsettled by such an attitude, he felt: men have their own whims but the hurly-burly of human society cannot be annulled or excommunicated without grave danger to the one who tries to do that. Those whose long-time abodes have been monasteries or even jails are seen afterwards, by those who happen to encounter them, to be maimed in mind and heart, often irrevocably. At least that was his impression but honesty made him concede that he had probably never met an individual who had that sort of past.

Two further calls were blank. One of them looked a bit promising at first, for in a quietish pub in the direction of the station he found himself drinking in the company of one who, judging from his dress, language and demeanour, was a Protestant clergyman. Mick was not skilled in discerning the various shades of the Reformed spectrum, and any personal enquiry on the point would be unmannerly. It was clear enough, however, that he was definitely not Joyce. He was courtly (and, be it added, quite sober) and invited Mick to have a drink with him before the latter had a chance to order his own. He was saying as the sherry arrived:

– It'll kill this young State if they're not careful.

– What – whiskey?

– Income tax. I'm convinced it's an immoral form of taxation.

– Does that mean that paying income tax is sinful?

– Well, no. In conscience one is entitled to choose the lesser of two evils. But heavy income tax ruins enterprise and initiative, and ultimately begets despondency and national decay.

– It is widely accepted, Mick reminded him, that this country has for centuries been subjected to vicious over-taxation and exploitation, both by the British Government and a cabal of corrupt and pitiless ruffians called absentee landlords. The Famine was one result of that régime.

– Ah there were bad times in the past.

– And I don't offend your reverence, I hope, by bringing to mind the horror of the tithes, when a beggared peasantry were compelled to support a Church in which they had no belief and for which they had no use.

– Quite, quite. And at a time when their own priests were hunted and persecuted.

– Yes, indeed.

– But ... *but*, I repeat, the remedy for all such old, indefensible evils is not this outrageous income tax. Not only is it bad of itself but it is quite unsuitable for this country's economy.

Such was their theme as Mick ordered his own two drinks in turn. He found the talk arid and useless.

When he withdrew he walked a good distance to the other end of town – almost to the outskirts, indeed, in the direction of Rush. Public houses can usually be trusted not to disguise themselves but he had almost passed one when only the rasping sound of a cork-puller alerted him. The low roof was thatched and inside, in the slow light of trimmed oil lamps peaceable men were drinking, mostly pints of porter. Conversation was casual and low-pitched and somehow Mick felt that many of the customers were retired fishermen. He asked the resident authority, a neat youngish man, for his little amber drink, and was surprised to hear him say 'It's a brave evenin',' indicating an origin in the far north.

Mick felt tired but still watchful. The lamplight was soft, agreeable, restful as gaslight, but suddenly he thought he heard a voice say something in a tone that made him start. Beyond a partition on the customers' side he saw another man serving within the counter further up the shop. He was oldish, thin, slightly stooped, and he wore glasses. Thick grey hair was brushed back from the forehead. Mick's heart began to thunder. Sweet God, *had he found James Joyce?*

He finished his drink, carefully and in recollection, and then went seeking the lavatory, always to be found in the rear of a house facing the street. On his return he paused at the back part of the shop. The elderly man came forward insecurely, blinking behind his thick glasses.

– A small pale sherry, please.

– Certainly.

He was neat and quiet in his movements as he went about fetching the drink. Would he talk readily, Mick wondered. Well, the job was to find out.

– Fairly large crowd in town, he said pleasantly. But whether it's really large or not I'm not so sure, as I'm a rare visitor, I'm sorry to say.

The reply was in the Dublin intonation, quite unmixed, and friendly as if in a true gentleness of nature.

— Ah, I think the town is doing all right this year. Of course, we're at the quiet end here, and thank God for that.

— You are a native, I suppose?

— No, no. No indeed.

Mick toyed with his glass, showing nonchalance.

— My own little trip to Skerries, he remarked, isn't really for the purpose of holiday. I came here looking for somebody who's in the town, I believe.

— A relative?

— No. A man I admire very much, a writer.

— Ah. I see?

— My good sir, I will not be so presumptuous as to ask you your name. Instead, I will tell you what it is.

The weak eyes seemed to grope behind their glass walls.

— Tell me . . . my name?

— Yes. Your name is James Joyce.

It was as if a stone had been dropped from a height into a still pool. The body stiffened. He put a hand about his face nervously.

— Quiet, please! Quiet! I am not known by that name here. I insist that you respect my affairs.

The voice was low but urgent.

— Of course I will, Mr Joyce. I shall mention no name again. But it is a really deep pleasure to meet a man of your attainments face to face. Your name stands high in the world. You are a most remarkable writer, an innovator, Dublin's incomparable archivist.

— Ah now, don't be talking like that.

— But I mean it.

— I have had a hurried sort of a life. Hither and thither you understand. The last war was a very unfortunate affair for everybody. Neither things nor people will ever be the same. The Hitler reign was an abominable thing. Ah yes, people suffered.

He was speaking freely now in a muted voice and there was a hint, perhaps, of relief.

– I think we all felt its impact, Mick said, even here in Ireland, far from the scene of it. I think at least one more sherry would do me good.

– Of course.

– And will you honour me by having a drink with me?

– No indeed, thank you. I take an occasional drink but not here, of course.

He served from the bottle.

– Your references to my work are kindly, he said, but I may mention that my real work has hardly appeared at all yet. Also, I've had things imputed to me which – ah – I've had nothing to do with.

– Is that so?

– The interruptions in Europe set me back a lot. I lost valuable papers.

– Those are serious drawbacks.

– The dear knows they are.

– Have you a new book in the process of ... incubation? Are you writing something new?

He gave a short, brief smile.

– Writing is not quite the word. Assembly, perhaps, is better – or accretion. The task I have set myself could probably be properly termed the translation into language of raw spiritual concepts. I stress here *translation* as distinct from *exposition*. It is a question of conveying one thing in terms of another thing which is ... em ... quite incongruous.

– Well, I'm sure that is difficult. Yet you have never faltered in conveying subtle or abstract things.

– Faith and that is very complimentary. But I have published little.

Mick decided to change direction.

– You are the second great pioneer I have had the good fortune to know.

– Well well now. And who is my nabs when he is at home?

133

– His name is De Selby. He is not a literary man so far as I know and it is not easy at all to define his sphere or spheres. He is a mathematical physicist, a chemist, an authority on dynamics and has achieved some astonishing conclusions in the time-space speculation. In fact he seems to have succeeded in interfering with the passing or flow of time. I'm sorry if I appear a bit incoherent but he seems to be able to make time go backwards. And he is also a theologian.

Joyce was showing, by intentness, his interest.

– This De Selby, he said. Where does he live?

– Near Dalkey, if you know where that is.

– Ah, Dalkey? Yes. Interesting little place. I know it well.

– He lives alone, in a very quiet house among the trees on the Vico Road. For all his intellect he is a courteous and hospitable man. Nothing of the mad scientist, you know.

Joyce, his curiosity now well kindled, was thinking.

– That is interesting, yes. Does he also teach or is he a university person?

– No, I don't think so. I don't think he has any job, in the usual sense. He never mentions money but that's possibly because he's plenty of it.

Joyce stared downward, reflecting.

– Wealthy, gifted, free to follow his fancy? It is well for him.

Mick liked this sympathetic thought.

– I had always thought of yourself, he said earnestly, as belonging to that sort of company. Your work seems to lack a sense of hurry – ungainly explosions, artificial tension and that sort of thing. You are not artificial. You understand me?

– Oh no, my position is not quite that. Scientific endeavour is, of course, good. Our family was preoccupied with politics, God help them, and with a little bit of music sometimes.

– Yes, but all these things are things of the mind. De Selby's scientific investigations don't preclude an interest in more abstract matters. Indeed, I am certain he would be delighted to meet yourself . . .

Joyce gave a low chuckle.

134

– Meet myself? Goodness now! He might not thank you for that suggestion.

– But seriously–

– You see, my work is very personal in the sense that much of the material is in my head. I'm afraid it could not be shared, and that nobody could help me. But of course it is always a pleasure to meet a person of quality.

– I understand. Has your new book got a name yet?

– No. I'm rather at sea as to *language*. I have a firm grip of my thoughts, my argument . . . but communicating the ideas clearly in English is my difficulty. You see, there has been considerable variation as between English on the one hand, and Hebrew and Greek as vehicles of epistemology.

– I know, of course, that you're interested in languages as such . . .

– My thoughts are new, you understand, and I'm afraid . . .

– What's the trouble?

– They tend to be ineffable.

– Dear me. But we talk in abstractions. I would like to get down to something hard and real for a moment and talk about *Finnegans Wake*.

Joyce started slightly.

– Good Lord! Do you know it? It was a well-known song in my young days.

– No, I meant the book.

– I did not know it was printed. Ah, once upon a time I was very fond of singing myself. The Irish airs, the ballads and the old come-all-ye's. When my heart was young, you might say.

– But surely you have heard of a book of that name – *Finnegans Wake*?

– You must remember, please, that I have been out of this country for a long time. If somebody has made an opera out of the old tunes, I am delighted, I wish him well. Tom Moore has always attracted me. 'Oft in the Stilly' is a beautiful song.

– Sentimental, yes.

– That is the usual thing to say, alas. That which touches one is dismissed as sentimental. The genuine old traditional airs, I like them very much too.

Was his mind wandering? Mick's watch told him that closing-time was near. He decided to stay the night in Skerries if necessary.

– Tell me this much, sir, he said. Would you mind if I told De Selby of our conversation without saying where you are, and suggest that you go to Dalkey for a meeting with him, or meet him here or somewhere else you think suitable?

Joyce paused in thought, nervously rubbing the counter with a finger. Possibly things were moving too fast. He frowned slightly.

– I would like to meet the man if you assure me he is discreet, he replied slowly, but I would not like to have him come here.

– I understand.

– He seems a curious man. It is perhaps just possible that he might be able to help me get what I have in mind down on paper, because the invention and involution this work calls for strains a single apparatus of reason. It is the sort of morass of problem and innovation on which the beam of a fresh mind might conceivably throw some light.

– You will not find De Selby's mind infertile or fixed in any mould.

– I am sure of that.

– Could you suggest a date and time of meeting him say at Dalkey?

– That's premature, I'm afraid. I must first have another talk with yourself.

– All right. I can stay here in the hotel tonight and see you bright and early tomorrow morning.

– No. I won't be here at all tomorrow. It's my day off. But before seeing your friend I want to have a long talk with yourself because there are certain things which have to be explained at the outset. I am a man who is much mis-understood – I will say maligned, traduced, libelled and slandered. From what I've heard, certain ignorant men in America have made a laugh of me. Even my poor father wasn't safe. A fellow named Gorman wrote that 'he always wore a monocle in one eye.' Fancy!

– I heard of that sort of thing myself.

– It is intolerable.

– I should not worry about such people.

– Ah, easy to say. Even here, where my identity is quite unknown, I'm regarded as a humbug, a holy Mary Ann, just because I go to daily Mass. If there's one thing scarce in Catholic Ireland, it is Christian charity.

Mick bowed his head in sympathy.

– I must agree with you, he said. We are a very mixed people. But . . . if I'm to get a train back to Dublin tonight, I must leave now, since I've quite a walk to the station. A further meeting tomorrow is out of the question. Very well. What other day do you suggest?

– I think we will have to wait a little bit and meet some-where other than here. Tuesday morning next week would suit me.

– Yes. That hotel in the town seems a reasonable clean place. I suppose they have a bar. Would that suit?

Joyce was silent for a moment, stooped.

– Well, yes . . . I suggest the back room at noon.

– Very good. And I have your permission to tell De Selby that I've met you and mention the possibility of some literary collaboration?

– Well, I suppose so.

– Sir, goodbye until Tuesday, and very many thanks.

– God bless you.

14

Mick's late-night return from Skerries faced him with an empty day on the morrow, though he left the house as if going to the office as usual. Instinct bade him keep away from Dalkey, where important work was to face him on the approaching Friday. What was he to do with himself on this spare-day?

First he made his way to St Stephen's Green and sought a seat there – easy enough so early in the morning. The Green is a railed-in square pleasure ground near the city centre, an extravagance of flower beds and fountains. A pretty lake, spanned at the centre by a bridge and having little islands, was the home of water fowl, many exotic and matching the flowers in hue and life. And the Green was constantly travelled by a great number of people since it offered a short cut diagonally between Earlsfort Terrace, where University College stood, and the top of Grafton Street – the portal of busy central Dublin. Curiously, this haven of hubbub (for that is what it sometimes seemed) was a good place for reflection and planning, as if all its burbling life was an anæsthesia, perhaps in the manner of finding loneliness in crowds.

He leaned back, closed his eyes, and meditated on what seemed to be his portion of things to be done. There were several things but, if big, they were not really complicated or unmanageable. He rather admired his own adroit manipulation of matters which, in certain regards, transcended this world. He would put a stop to the diabolical plans of De Selby, for instance, but by means of what was no less than comic-opera subterfuge. Again, Mick had been the one to be in a position to demonstrate that James Joyce, a writer and artist of genius, was not dead as commonly supposed but alive and reasonably well in the country of his birth. True, his card had been marked in this regard by the loquacious and bibulous Dr Crewett but Mick doubted if the latter himself believed the information he had given; at all events he had made no attempt to verify it. Perhaps sheer laziness was the explanation, and Mick was pleased to reflect that sloth was not a sin that could be laid at his own door.

No indeed, for if anybody was active and alert it was Mick. Apart from having had a physical confrontation with Joyce, he had discovered that his mind was unbalanced. He did not realize that he had finished and published *Finnegans Wake*, for it was too ridiculous to suppose that some sort of a draft, yet to be worked upon, had got into print accidentally without his knowledge. Publishers, Mick knew, were not given to irresponsible tomfoolery, particularly where an important established name was concerned. Yet Joyce betrayed no eccentricity of manner or speech in that pub in Skerries, and went about that job in which Mick so unexpectedly found him with composure and efficiency. Was De Selby off his rocker as well and, if so, how would two exquisitely cultivated but distracted minds behave on impact with each other? Would they coalesce in some quiet and fruitful way, or clash in murderous disarray? Was Mick getting a bit misdirected in the head himself in planning to bring those two men together? Well, hardly. De Selby had given him no overt sign of insanity but on the contrary had given him proof, in that meeting with St Augustine, that his powers and contacts were at least preternatural. Mick could not possibly run any risk about the reality of the D.M.P. threat. He had, bluntly, an obligation to the human race, one that could not be gainsaid by an extremity of cowardice or casuistry.

But Mick's imagination would not be quiet. Would Joyce and De Selby combine their staggeringly complicated and diverse minds to produce a monstrous earthquake of a new book, something claiming to supplant the Bible? De Selby could easily produce the incredible materials, perhaps with the help of angels, while Joyce could supply the unearthly skill of the master-writer. The answer here seemed to be that De Selby had no interest in literature or neo-theology, or in doing anything to improve or embellish this world or its people: his aim was to destroy both, with himself and Joyce included in this prodigious annihilation.

Supposing Mick's introduction of Joyce to De Selby co-incided with the latter's discovery that his cask was missing, what would happen then? Would he blame Joyce and murder him? That would be most unfortunate, to say the least of it, and it probably would be impossible for Mick to disavow (at least to himself) his personal share in this blood-shed. Yes, his affairs were ringed with risk: the situation could not be otherwise. And it was too late to go back in the case of De Selby, though in theory Mick could leave Joyce where he was and forget forever the little town of Skerries. Even that was not certain as a possibility, for he had be-trayed to Joyce the name of De Selby and his dwelling at Dalkey, and Joyce could well appear on the scene, of his own motion. That would be a detestable development, for it would mean that matters were getting outside Mick's per-sonal control. It seemed clear that he must keep his second appointment with Joyce in Skerries; the movements of a man whose brain was disorganized were unpredictable but it was possible he could be managed by contrived, perhaps unscrupulous, persuasion. But was that man Joyce at all? Could one reputedly so contemptuous of God be now so unusually pious, so meticulous in his observance of his duties as a member of the Church? How could such an attitude, admittedly a later one, be reconciled with the intricate and bombastic scatology of *Ulysses* and, even in an interval of aberration, so base a character as Molly Bloom?

Ah, Molly Bloom! Should he use this free and easy day to contact Mary, perhaps ring her at her Boutique or whatever she called it? He found himself frowning. A sort of numbness crept over him. He had been thinking loosely and emotionally rather than exactly. He sternly told himself to behave rationally and to see to it that when decisions were made, they were sound as well as irrevocable.

The elderly man in Skerries *was* Joyce, with certain departments of his mind upset by experience amid the horror of Nazi Europe. He had not disclaimed literary work but, in his strange job as barman – probably very temporary – he could be forgiven for not dwelling on his past preoccupations. What of his exemplary life as a son of the Church? This was a question that touched on the psychological, the psychotic, perhaps the theological. In such country Mick felt hardly qualified to make judgement: indeed, who could overlook the famous quandary of Saint Paul?

If in fact after a second interview with Joyce an arrangement was made for him to meet De Selby, Mick would have by that time the way made ready. Two elderly men, of giant intellectual potential, who had run wild somewhat in their minds might, in coming together, find a community of endeavour and unsuspected common loyalties. Both certainly knew what whiskey was. Mick wondered whether in the absence of his deadly container De Selby could continue to produce perfectly mature whiskey which was only seven days old? Could one look forward to the founding of the firm of De Selby, Joyce & Co., distillers, maltsters and warehousemen, to market those high-grade spirits all over the world and make a fortune? Mick smiled at this, again chiding his mind for erupting into fancy.

Then Mary. Well, why should he meet her or even ring her up on this free day of his? He had long thought, or taken it for granted, that he was deeply, hopelessly in love with Mary. Was he? Infatuation is a weakness one readily attributes to other people but his mounting honesty with himself made him stare this awkward question straight. First, Mary was indefatigable in probing and catechizing him, even in matters which were strictly his own business. She was very careful to underline her independence of him as male escort and was quite unrestrained in expressing her own ideas on art, manners, customs, even politics and the rest of the human equipage. Her *own* ideas? How home-made in fact were they? No doubt glossy magazines abounded in her little palace of fashion, and the art of learning to talk smart was no new one. Probably she could manage brief quotes from Mallarmé or Voltaire when the feat seemed opportune. A reasonable case could be made for establishing that in fact she despised him. What was she, really, but a gilded trollop, probably with plenty of other gents who were devout associates. Or slaves, marionettes?

In recent times his unprecedented contacts with persons (or beings) quite out of the ordinary had tended to direct all his cerebral attention outward, never inward at his own self. This was an unjustified lapse, plain neglect. He could not hope to counter adequately the moves of others if the nature of himself and his own strength were not in every particular known to him – familiar to him, even. Every man must know how to deploy his forces, all his forces. De Selby was a case in point. Hackett and Mick himself had assumed he had been lying about D.M.P. and his power of suspending time, but he had proved he was not. It was a fact that he had powers not commonly understood, that he was infinitely crafty, and that he was as ready to lie as anybody on minor matters. He was also skilled in saying absolutely nothing about mundane simple matters in a way which would arouse the curiosity of the most stolid – e.g. where did he get his money? He had to eat and drink, buy apparatus and chemicals, even pay the poor rate. Where did he get the common coin to meet such unavoidable if prosaic obligations? If he were living on a fortune already made – well, made of what? Was he a bank-robber from the U.S.A., quietly thriving on an immense haul, possibly after he had gunned down his associates rather than share with them? If De Selby was an enigma, his peculiar aura was that of an evil enigma.

But Mick noted that his own function and standing had risen remarkably. He was *supervising* men of indeterminate calibre, of sanity that was more than suspect. Clearly enough this task had been assigned to him by Almighty God, and this gave him somewhat the status of priest. He was certainly as much a priest as Father Cobble, whom both De Selby and himself had dismissed as stupid. True, Mick lacked regular ecclesiastical faculties but that was a matter that could be attended to with time. A blessed plant must be conceded an interval of ungainliness, awkward and coarse striving, before an enchanting bloom exuding salvational odour could be expected to burst upon the world. He did think – though afterwards he could not be sure – that it was during this afternoon in St Stephen's Green that it first dawned on him that he should join the Church's ministry and labour as best he might in the old vineyard.

He got up and walked abstractedly about winding pathways. His mood was a formless one of renunciation. What about his mother? That grand lady was old, decayed enough so far as health went. And she had a younger sister, also a widow but comfortably off, in Drogheda. No, separation from his old mother would be no obstacle and the knowledge that he was becoming a priest would shine over her closing years, like a blessed candle.

One other thing. He was spending far too much of his free money on drink. He was by no means a soak or debauché, that was certain. The curse about pubs was that they were so ubiquitous and accessible. If one had something to discuss with another person in Dublin, whether the subject was trivial or critical, inevitably the appointment was made for a public house. The thing was a social malaise, a neurotic flaw in community development, a situation in which the unreliable quality of the climate was perhaps a big factor. There were tea-rooms, of course, coffee-palaces, even lounges in some hotels where a gracious glass of sherry would be forthcoming. Somehow they were each an unsuitable milieu for colloquy between men – and by no means because the pint of porter was not to be had. To say there is a time and a place for everything is trite, but the truth of the sentiment is not to be denied for all that; one could play the accordion while having a bath but probably nobody has ever tried to do that. He abruptly sat down on a seat quite elsewhere in the Green but the beautiful, featureless scene looked the same: people hurrying, birds flying, scurrying and shrieking and a solitary peacock mooching in the shadows at some low shrub. Was there not a futility about what was nice and orderly?

His association with Mary, now that he contemplated it soberly, had been really very superficial and small; perhaps banal would be the juster word. Certainly it had not been sinful and there was nothing at all in it of the sort of conduct he associated with the name of Hackett. He would put an end to the thing with no loss to himself but not too abruptly and certainly with no parade of bad manners. It is really easy to let allegiances, no longer held, lapse.

He kicked idly away a little stone at his foot. Let's see now – which order? Happily, any doubt here was only in detail. To join the ordinary secular clergy was unthinkable, for it would entail spending many years in Maynooth College, an institution founded by the British Government to prevent aspiring Irish clerics from getting their training and education in such centres as Paris and Louvain. He would emerge therefrom as a C.C. or 'Catholic Curate' and possibly be assigned to some such parish as Swanlinbar. He said it with sorrow, and God forgive him for saying it at all, but the great majority of C.C.s he had met were ignorant men, possibly schooled in the mechanics of ordinary theology but quite unacquainted with the arts, not familiar with the great classical writers in Latin and Greek, immersed in a swamp of tastelessness. Still, he supposed they could be discerned as the foot-soldiers of the Christian army, not to be examined individually too minutely.

Obviously he was an enclosed order man. Which order?

Hard to say. His feeling, not yet properly formed, seemed to tend in the direction of the more severe and monastic orders, though – here one may smile forbearingly – he did not in fact know how many such orders there were and how their rule differed in severity. One thing he was fairly sure of: the Order of Saint John of God entailed a vow of silence for life. Somehow in the genial rowdiness of the Green this seemed a petty enough liability to embrace. What was wrong with a bit of peace for a change? The Cistercians were good men, too, he believed, and the Carthusians. He felt vaguely that the term 'enclosed order' was a bit misleading and perhaps misunderstood. It did not mean complete monastic seclusion, pitilessly frugal diet, being awakened from plank beds in the middle of the night to say the office, and being attired during working hours in the roughest and least elegant of robes. There were, of course, true monks of that heroic stamp but he took leave to question whether such a regimen was not sinfully wasteful. *Laborare est orare*, yes, but the contrary was hardly true. Look at the Holy Ghost Fathers. They were an enclosed order as far as he knew but they taught school, the Fathers were eligible for bishoprics in the common outside Church and they engaged also, he thought, in foreign mission. He realized sadly that he was terribly ignorant of the structure, organization and government of the universal Church. Remote indeed was his prospect of ever becoming Pope.

In all this formless contemplation his eyes were open, thrown towards the ground but sightless. Yet vision came back when two blackish objects, not too clean, came towards him. They were a pair of shoes, occupied. His eyes lifted to the round, beaming face of a character whom he knew as Jack Downes. The face was pleasant and seemed to say that it had been formed somewhere down the country where abided comely cows, lazy fertile sows, and homely hens of the pristine egg. He was perhaps twenty-two, a medical student and, the Dublin phrase, 'a hard chaw'. This phrase was undeserved, for it suggests that one is forever loitering about, playing cards, drinking, interfering with girls and doing absolutely anything except opening a book or attending a lecture. Mick knew that Downes had already impeccably traversed three years of the medical course. His equal readiness to ingest the secrets of physic and pints of plain porter puzzled many people, not excluding Hackett, who sometimes mentioned the Downes Syndrome, being 'that degree of stupidity which can produce information irrelevant to the question asked but imparted with such elaboration and *appoggiatura* that the querist rarely risks saying the answer is wrong'. That was unfair, too, but Mick's opinion had long been that university studies were a barren activity. Dublin's two university colleges were choked with the sons of dishonest country publicans.

– Well, by the damn, Downes growled jovially, what are you doing hiding here, you long-faced sleeveen?

– Morra, Jack. I'm just taking a rest and minding my own business.

– For God's sake? It's nearly twelve. You're about three hours out of bed, and you're resting yourself? Why the hell aren't you earning your living or at least in some chapel saying a Hail Mary for the Holy Souls? I suppose you still call yourself an Irishman. A gobdaw is what I'd call you, Michael.

– Oh, cut it out, Mick said rather testily. It's a bit early in the morning for your big, broad, ignorant Paddy Whack stuff, and I don't want irreligious guff from you at any time.

– Ah-ha? Something's biting you.

He then made the last gesture of succour that was looked for. He sat down.

– Never mind, he said in a tone meant to be gentle, just take it easy and you'll find what you think are troubles will just evaporate. Do you understand Planck's quantum theory?

– I don't.

146

– Right. No points then in talking about ERGS. Do you know where Chatham Street is?

– Of course I do.

– That's better. That street is quite near and in it is an excellent house called Neary's. If you will arise, rely on my strong arm, I will lead you to it, and there buy you a pint. To tell you the truth, I need one myself.

– Well, that's a good reason for going there.

There was a trace of real dismay in Mick's voice when he looked at Downes. This invitation was athwart the preceding reverie.

– Jack, isn't it a bit early in the day to start that game? By half-one we'd be putting smahans of malt into ourselves.

– Not a bit of it. No fear at all of that. Anyway, I want to talk to you. We'd be overheard if we talked in a place like this.

– When's your next exam?

– November. Plenty of time.

– Wouldn't you be better occupied getting a theory or two into your head than getting porter into your belly?

– That's hard to say. Let's get going.

He stood up in a way that was jaunty yet a bit peremptory. What could Mick do? He was now in a neutral humour. He stood up too and they strolled out of the Green to Grafton Street and were soon in Neary's, an unhurried, secluded refuge. Jack Downes ordered two pints without the formality of asking what Mick's choice was, and he demolished nearly half of his own when it arrived, in one great swallow. He put his feet up on a nearby chair.

– Tell me, Mick, avic, he said solicitously, just what sort of trouble are you in?

Mick gave a little chuckle.

– Trouble? You are the one who first mentioned it. I'm not in any trouble that I know of.

– Good Lord! You looked so desolate sitting there in the Green, like a bereaved scarecrow.

147

– Well, I have one little item of trouble, but easily susceptible of remedy, I think. Constipation.

– Oh, hell, Downes said disdainfully, sure everybody has that. It's like Original Sin. But look at me. *I'm* in real trouble.

– What's wrong?

– Plenty. I have to be at Kingsbridge Station this evening shortly after six to meet a train. Th'oul fella's coming up to visit me.

– Well isn't that all right? I know that you get on well with your father and I know he's not backward in coming forward with a grant-in-aid on such visits. And your College record is clear.

Downes grunted.

– Look, he said, there has been a bloody complication. Last time he was here, he produced his gold watch, priceless family heirloom, and said there was something wrong with it. We went together to a certain watchmaker, and this genius quickly found out what the trouble was. He quoted a price, which the oul fella paid. I was to collect the watch in a week and keep it safe and sound.

– And did you?

– Yes and no. I collected it all right and it was going and in first class order. Soon I did a very stupid thing.

– Don't tell me you lost it?

– No. I pawned it.

Mick was slowly managing his unwanted pint as he heard those words. Weren't people truly very foolish, himself included?

– Where did you pawn it? he finally asked.

– In Meredith's of Cuffe Street.

That was the accepted pawnshop for university students. Mick pondered the situation. He did not think it a grave one.

– How much did you get on it?

– Two pounds ten. That's all I asked.

– Where's the pawn ticket?

– I have it here.

148

After a search he produced what looked like the genuine ticket.

– My terrible trouble, Downes said dismally, is that I'm dead broke. Broke to the wide. First thing the daddy will look for is the watch. With no watch, he'll kick up buggery and melia murder. He could make a holy show of me in the station.

– I met him briefly only once. He's not as bad as all that.

– He could be worse when it's a question of that watch. I can't even think up any kind of a story.

Mick emitted a brief laugh.

– If you look at this situation squarely, he intoned, you'll find it's really very simple. Your College affairs are in order and I know your landlady is paid direct, in advance. Your good father will give you an *ex gratia* gift of ten pounds for your good luck. All you have to do is borrow the money to redeem the watch, with your borrowed money outstanding only for a matter of hours. Simple!

– Borrow? But where? I'd need three quid.

– Surely you have a few friends? Ah-ha now, you needn't look at me. Our glasses are empty and it's my turn to buy a drink. And I'm going to have a Vichy water this time.

He gestured at a curate and gave the order, at the same time taking out in his hand all the money in his right trousers pocket – three half crowns and smaller coins. He held forward this sample.

– On my word of honour, Jack, he said seriously, that's absolutely all the money I have on me.

Downes gave the collection a troubled glance.

– I know, he said. A year ago I borrowed twenty-five bob offa the landlady to buy a present for my young sister on the occasion of her Confirmation. I couldn't go there again, of course, though I paid the money back. I have an idea that she got to know I haven't any sister.

As the drinks arrived he fell silent and glum, while Mick began to settle the little matter in his mind. Jack Downes was a decent fellow when all was said, and worth helping. There seemed one obvious course to take, though it involved slight risk to his own financial equilibrium. Jack's salvation was in his pocket: the cheque-book, as yet unused.

In all his muddling supernatural and scientific diversions, Mick reminded himself, he must not lose sight of that true manifestation of humanity's nobility – *compassion*. Beside it any other virtue was shallow and poor. Love and pity were other names for it, or in Latin *caritas*, charity. Even the brute creation was not entirely without it. And if he risked the loss of £3, was it not a cheap way of easing a distressed mind, preventing family rupture and perpetuating conditions that were happy and leading to permanent achievement in another man's life?

Yes, his duty was plain enough. Yet a little caution was called for. There could be no question of writing out a cheque there and then and handing it over. There was an impetuous element in the character of Jack Downes. Any operation Mick started he would have to supervise to the end. He spoke at last.

– Jack, he said, it's quite true that what I showed you is all the money I have. Indeed, I could do with a quid myself in view of certain small expenses I foresee in a day or two. It happens that I have a tiny hidden horde of savings – *tiny*, I repeat, but there to be called upon in an emergency . . .

Downes had been looking at him blankly, and then gave a sort of smile.

– You mean—

– I mean that I have a cheque-book. I will now make out a cheque payable to Bearer and we will walk down to the Bank of Ireland. You will then go into the bank and cash the cheque, writing your name on the back. I will wait outside. When you come out, you will hand me the money, and then we can see what can be done about that watch.

Very pleasing was the effect this simple, generous speech

had on Downes. His face became slightly illuminated, and his person exuded geniality.

— Mick, you are a strange sort of an angel in need of a shave, a heavenly witch-doctor.

Mick wrote the cheque, and of this tale there is little more to tell. As Downes disappeared into the bank, Mick wondered whether there would be any question about what was his first cheque ever. Well, there wasn't. Very soon, four clean banknotes were in his hand.

— Next stop, Jack, is Meredith's. We'll walk.

Within half an hour they paused to part. Jack had a venerable half-hunter watch in his pocket as well as some change out of £3. He was loud on the subject of repayment but Mick cut him short and told him to be sure and meet the father that evening. When free, he hurried into an underground restaurant and had strong black coffee and buns. Was it not the sort of repast, he reflected, which behoved the good Samaritan? A newspaper which he bought he found unreadable. He felt confused but happy, and resolutely thrust all thoughts of Mary, De Selby and even Joyce out of his head. Things must be taken in turn, and quietly. What now? He walked into a cinema without bothering to see what was advertised. It was half-price before 5 p.m.

When he got home at the usual time, he felt hungry.

— You look tired, his mother remarked. Another hard day?

— Ah yes, mother, he said, slumping into a chair. Some of those people from down the country can be very troublesome.

15

Mick was punctual enough when at 8.40 p.m. he pushed open the door of the police station in Dalkey on that Friday night. At last action was to take the place of dialogue and dissertation. He returned the salutation of Policeman Pluck who, seated in the dayroom, had contorted his red features into that pucker which was intended for a smile.

– Ah but that's the fine evening, he chuckled, if a man had the time off to mosey up to Larkin's for a couple of cruiskeens of porter, or maybe a talk with that grand dark lump of a girl from Longford that the P.P. keeps hidden in his kitchen, be the holy powers!

Mick nodded pleasantly.

– Yes, Mr Pluck, but some people have other things to think of. The sergeant and myself are thinking about getting the people around interested in bicycle-racing. A fine healthy sport.

– They will have to take an engineering course in punctures for themselves, he muttered. The Big Wig is inside there at the back.

– Thanks.

Sergeant Fottrell was indeed in what he called his office, kneeling at his bicycle making some adjustment. His bicycle-clips were on.

– Gracious greeting, he said, glancing up.

– Are you ready for the winding trail, Sergeant?

– We are ready and awake, he replied, but in the dire emergency I have had to borrow Policeman Pluck's pump.

– What? Surely you are not going to bring the bicycle with you?

The sergeant stood up and looked at Mick searchingly.

– We are on a rarefied secret business tonight, he said in a confidential tone, and we want nobody to be showering obnoxious attentions on us contemptuously. For me to go out on the roads or streets of this parish without my bicycle would be worse than going out without my trousers on me.

– Well, I know, but . . .

– I have never appeared in public without my bicycle, though that is not to say that I was ever so vexed a fool as to get up on it.

Mick realized that here was no question of etiquette but of discipline tender as steel. Clearly his own role was to be adroit, diplomatic. The thing was to get De Selby's container and hide it overnight as unnoticeably as possible. Argument or contention was unthinkable.

– Of course, Sergeant. I quite realize that a bicycle wheeled by one's side is a form of disguise. I quite approve. But one thought has just crossed my mind.

– Ah, a micro-wave? And what is that?

– I've just remembered that you have *my* bicycle locked up in one of the cells. Would it be a proper thing for me to wheel mine?

The sergeant frowned. The point was apparently a knotty one in cycle liturgy. Mick bit his lip.

– Well, no, the sergeant said slowly. You are in pure divine essence a personality who *rides* a bicycle when he has any intercourse with it at all. But I am of a disfamiliar persuasion. I have never been on top of a bicycle in my life and never will be, world without end.

– Very well, Mick agreed. Let us get going. Let us keep to our timetable.

And they did set out – but by the back door, without the cognisance of Policeman Pluck.

Dusk had long since gathered and they made scarcely any notable spectacle in the little streets of Dalkey, ill-lit by uneven gas-lamps and almost void save for the muted noises and flood of light from an occasional public house, giving notice that life was still intact. Soon they were at the beginning of the gentle climb of the Vico Road. They had long

153

passed the Colza Hotel without mention of it or an acknowledgement by either of them that it was there. Sergeant Forttrell's comportment was casual, secretive, silent. Mick would be happier if the sergeant were more at his ease and he began to talk to him conversationally in a low voice.

— Both of us, Sergeant, he said, are doing something useful and, I suppose, morally meritorious in depriving that man De Selby of the reservoir of deadly germs he is hoarding.

— It is ourselves we are honouring by our patrician prodigality, the Sergeant replied in what appeared to be concurrence. Mick grunted genially.

— Well, I want to tell you of a special personal sacrifice of my own. As you know, I am a civil servant.

— Splendour and strong arm, vessel of the State, the sergeant chanted.

— Ah well, we do our best. A civil servant has so-many days' leave a year. I have just three weeks. He may apply for it all in one bash, or take it in dribs and drabs.

— Or concisely in drabs and dribs, the sergeant suggested. The gentle clicking whisper of his bicycle was ever a shadow over their words.

— But remember, Mick continued, a day is a day and a day's leave is a day's leave. On Saturday work ends at one o'clock and most of us think of that day as a half day. So it is, I suppose. But there is no such thing as a half day's leave. Do you understand?

— I follow you meticulously.

— When we get this article of De Selby's and hide it near the road, it must be collected early tomorrow morning. To leave it there over the weekend would be a risk too appalling to contemplate for one half minute.

The sergeant made an assenting sort of groan.

— Nor a tenth of that. If the laden weight of this diabolical miracle of science was indicatively reasonable maybe we could bring it away on the crossbar of my bicycle and hide it under the bed in the station.

154

This suggestion, the climax of irresponsibility, horrified Mick.

– For heaven's sake, Sergeant, not on your life. That would leave humanity still open to the perils incubated by De Selby. Over the weekend Policeman Pluck might discover it when you were out and try to burst it open, thinking it was a cask of cider.

The sergeant chuckled sardonically.

– Father Cummins, the curate, is away in the County Tipperary visiting his sick mother. We could leave the thing by exiguous stealth inside his confession box in the church. No man subject to his senses would think of looking there for anything.

On the Vico Road they were nearing the tiny gap in the railings which gave access to De Selby's dwelling. Mick caused a halt by deterring the sergeant's bicycle. This was for emphasis.

– Sergeant Fottrell, he said in a hidden earnest voice, I have arranged this operation down to the smallest detail. We dare not depart from the plan. We will get De Selby's thing down to these railings, if necessary by rolling it, and hide it inside for the night. Early tomorrow morning a taxi will stop very near my own house and the driver will wait. When I join him, we will drive here, collect the thing and bring it to where it will be absolutely safe forever. Now isn't that simple?

They moved on, as the sergeant was not inclined to argue the point. He seemed to regard himself, very properly, as a professional adviser on house-breaking, undertaken in the public interest. And when they did reach the gap in the railings he was miraculously deft and fast in extinguishing his bicycle in the shrubs and foliage.

In a quite silent ascent through the trees, Mick carefully guided him by the sleeve. The house was completely in darkness, without the whisper of life from it. Its outline, with some detail, was quite perceptible as it stood in its strange clearing. The hall door was visible but offered no enticement to the sergeant who, now taking Mack by the sleeve, hugged the shadow of the trees and deviously led the way to the back.

Two smallish windows, each with two sashes of equal size, invited them. Their circuit of the house showed it to be surprisingly small and shallow in relation to its frontage.

The sergeant chose a window and produced a slim pocket-knife. He then tried to peer at the region of the catch, began handling the sides of the sash and to Mick's bewilderment, suddenly slid up the bottom one, without benefit of knife, to leave an aperture of about two feet by a foot and a half. Into this he inserted his big head and called softly:

– Is there anybody there? Is there anybody there?

No answer came from the gloom. He withdrew his head and used it to give Mick a gigantic nod. Then in through the aperture he inserted his large right leg and with swift very complicated contortions had the whole of himself inside. As Mick laboriously followed, he reflected that their foolhardy break-in was by no means in the pattern or pace of the underworld as set forth in books. Indeed, so far as he knew, neither of them was armed (if it is agreed not to take account of that knife in the sergeant's pocket). The sergeant carefully and quietly closed the window.

Mick produced a small torch of brilliant but very narrow beam and surveyed the apartment with its eye. They seemed to be in a clean neat sort of kitchen. There was a roughish, scrubbed table, cupboards, shelves with packets and tins on them, a refrigerator, a small electric cooker and a few chairs. These were the quarters of a careful person.

The closed door opened inward readily to Mick's hand and he called softly without result the sergeant's query of 'Is there anybody there?' It was simple to head towards the front of the house, traversing a short passage and arriving in the hall. He guided the sergeant into the sitting-room which the torch soon revealed to be empty. There were some newspapers on the floor and a rug hung from the side of an armchair. On the mantelpiece was a pot and a small cup showing signs of dribble. He went straight to the press with the key between his fingers. The dull metal cask was there, just as he had last seen it. He gestured to the sergeant and silently handed him the torch. The cask tilted readily enough from side to side but he found it difficult, in his kneeling position, to lift it. He pulled at it, sliding it outward. There was a drop of an inch from the bottom of the press to the floor, and it fell outwards towards him on its side, on the thinly carpeted floor. Its construction, beautifully exact, was such that it rested on its median circumference, both extremities being clear of the floor. He rolled it some distance from the press, which he then re-locked. He stood up, took the torch from the sergeant, and motioned him to lift the cask and put it on the table. This the sergeant quickly and easily did.

It was clear enough now that a slight relaxation of caution was permissible.

– Is it heavy? Mick whispered.

– Not at all, came a piercing whisper which might be heard in Dalkey, just about the weight of a month-old sheep by the holy hokey.

Why didn't he say a month-old lamb? Mick tried lifting the cask himself. He was surprised, for it belied its massive appearance. He thought it about the weight of a medium-sized typewriter.

– We'll carry it turn about, he whispered, with myself always in front on that difficult track through the trees. We'll go out through the hall door. We must go carefully and slowly. You carry first. I'll open and close the door.

– Inferentially, the sergeant commented, laying strong arms about the prize.

Slow and meticulous was the descent to those railings by the roadside, momentous as the burden was, rapid its stowing away in the undergrowth. Though not a single tiny thing went wrong, Mick's heart kept thumping throughout the journey, and even afterwards, when he and the sergeant with his retrieved bicycle were casually walking down the Vico Road.

– Do you know, the sergeant said in a low confidential voice, do you know something? Do you know what is going to happen at six o'clock tomorrow morning?

– No – what? Mick asked, suddenly a bit scared. What very obvious thing had he overlooked?

– At six or thereabouts, the sergeant intoned, that west wind will bring on its cruel lip a whirlwind of downpours and contumelious cloudbursts to frighten out of their wits the poor farmers and gardeners who have still crops in the ground, slobbers of water fearful to behold.

This prophecy amused Mick a bit. Ever a forward looking man, the sergeant clearly regarded their own night's work as something done and finished with, a book closed, a meal eaten, a thing never to be mentioned again or even thought of. Mick's involute, hand-knitted, littered mind found such a compact, simple state of affairs indigestible but he was grateful that the sergeant saw things that way, for unconsciously his attitude was an accommodation of Mick's own strange preoccupation.

He played back the ball of weather-talk and was rewarded with short accounts of catastrophes in the far past arising from nature's inexcusable waywardness, the Irish potato-famine of the black eighteen-forties having been due to nothing else but weeks of the blackest frost in the history of mankind! They had reached the station and Mick was holding out a hand in thanks and goodbye when the sergeant guided him inwards by the shoulder.

– A skillet of tea would do the both of us good, he said in a tone intended to be that of wheedle, and pay no attention to Policeman Pluck's snotty snivelling about punctures.

Snivelling he pronounced snyvelling.

16

When Mick left the police station that night he was surprised to note that it was only slightly after ten o'clock. Against his judgement he decided to visit the Colza and offer his apology in person to De Selby. Readymade lies kept flocking into his head. His appointment that night had been for the purpose of fixing up an appointment with the eminent writer James Joyce. However, while in town he was passing by when a motor car knocked down and injured a cyclist. The police had insisted on his going along to the station and making a written statement as a witness. The police were hopelessly slow and incompetent. They had wrecked his evening on foot of an occurrence he had absolutely nothing to do with, and he could only apologize. He was extremely sorry.

The Colza Hotel could remain open to visitors until eleven but either elasticity of conscience or unreliability of time-pieces on the part of Mrs Laverty made closing time always uncertain. Sergeant Fottrell, the scourge of many a Dalkey publican, paid absolutely no attention to this house beyond occasionally drinking there. Anybody who got drunk there never coupled the offence with the other unthinkable offence of being disorderly.

It was ten-thirteen when Mick got there to find Hackett, a bit dim-eyed, in the bar, with Mrs L knitting behind the counter. Somehow he felt this whole night was tuned in a low key. He bade a general goodnight and sat at the counter. Mrs Laverty set about the surprising request for a bottle of Vichy water.

— Well, you have a great gift for being nearly in time, Hackett said somewhat unsteadily. Reminds me of your mother's disclosure to me that you were an eight-month baby. Your man departed only fifteen minutes ago.

Mick was not sure but perhaps he was relieved at this.

– Thanks, Hackett, he replied. I'm grateful for your co-operation. Actually it wouldn't have mattered in the least whether I'd met him.

– Did your own scheme work out according to plan?

– I think so, yes.

– And where have you put the property of the person of the first part?

– Ah, never mind. It doesn't matter. Somewhere very safe. We may worry about it no more.

Hackett resumed attending to his drink, frowning a little. He was moody, his temper uncertain. He motioned Mick to join him in a back seat in the Slum, and Mick obeyed.

– It's a pity you missed De Selby, Hackett said, because he wanted to meet you for his own reasons. He only hinted to me what they were. He said he knew you had certain suspicions about his intentions with that chemical he used in the Saint Augustine episode. He does not blame you but wanted you to know that he had completely changed his mind. He now admits that he had been under bad influence, pretty well subject to an exterior power. But by a miracle – or a series of them – his mind was cleared. He wanted you to be informed of that, and to stop worrying. 'Within a few days,' he said, 'I will make a most unambiguous retraction of my error. I will make an end of all my experiments and return as a peaceable citizen to Buenos Aires, where my good patient wife is waiting for me. I have plenty of money, honestly earned' . . .

Mick stared at him.

– That is astonishing talk, he said, and mystifying rather than enlightening. Can anybody believe a word De Selby says, or even understand it?

Hackett gestured to Mrs Laverty for a repeat medicament.

– The only direct contact I have had in any of this business, he said, is that of having been with you and De Selby in that meeting with Saint Augustine. But I have never been certain that it was not an hallucination, as I've told you before. De

Selby would be the last to deny that he is an accomplished witch-doctor. Very likely we were drugged. There is no limit to the drugs which induce fantasy.

– Hackett, we've discussed this before. No drug could induce an identical fantasy in two separate individuals. All branches of science – chemical, medical, psychological, neuropathic – are all agreed on that.

Hackett grumpily paid for the beaker Mrs Laverty had brought.

– Well listen here, he said, I wish to God I had never met that clown De Selby, and I told him so. I made it clear that I didn't like him and didn't want his Christmas pudding. But that was after he had revealed to me that he has a cell in his house sealed as tight as the sea ever sealed the underwater chamber at the Vico Swimming Club. Apparently he has been going into his domestic eternity wearing his breathing mask practically every day and conversing with the dead. It still seems to be exclusively with the heavenly dead, which seems odd in view of his other claim that he derives his powers from the Devil. What do you say?

– I don't know what to say. I haven't yet heard what his latest disclosures are.

Hackett nodded.

– I can only summarize what he said. One thing I forgot to tell you. He was properly plastered when he came here, and you said my job was to ply him with drink. My real job was to stop him nursing himself into a slumber of insensibility. Mrs L was getting very upset and when he left a quarter of an hour ago, it was in the care of Teague McGettigan. I had to send for the cab. The man was stotious.

Mick shook his head. This was indeed an unhappy, unforeseen diversion. He found it hard to assess its significance: possibly nil, for drunken ranting by a person of De Selby's standing could be macabre and frightening without really meaning anything or calling for serious notice. Still . . .

– No doubt he broke a rule, as we all do now and again, he

remarked, and started, a rash sampling of that special whiskey of his. Whom did he say he was seeing in that celestial laboratory of his?

Hackett began rummaging in his pocket.

– I tried to scribble down some names, he replied, but one man he seemed to be seeing practically every day was Augustine, as if he was a sort of chaplain in the house.

– Who else?

Hackett was frowning at a ragged piece of paper.

– I'm not sure about some of these names – my attempts were phonetic, mostly. Athenagoras, Ignatius of Antioch, Cyprian, John of Damascus . . .

– Goodness! He does not exclude the Greek Fathers?

– John Chrysostom, Theodore of Mopsuestia, Gregory of Nazianzus . . .

– Hackett, I confess that my own grasp of patrology is limited but what on earth would De Selby gain by dialogue with Fathers so diverse in origin and even in doctrine? But this time he seems to confine himself to the Fathers proper. I do know that the last of the reputed Fathers was Gregory the Great, who died somewhere around 600.

Hackett laughed. Alcohol had also left its inflexion on his mind and voice.

– We have often read, he said, that such-and-such a Royal Commission has power to send for persons and papers. Well, De Selby has power to send for parsons and papists. His summonses aren't always addressed to individuals to attend for a private collogue. Know whom he had down one morning?

– Who?

– A whole detachment – if that's the word – from the Council of Trent, including, he said, certain cardinals who tried to wreck the unhappy Council through the Pope's scheme to get the Council to denounce the Protestants as heretics.

Mick was aghast at such an excess.

– We must remember the man was drunk when he gave

out such extreme language to you, Hackett, he said.

Hacket nodded.

– And you could say that I wasn't too sober listening to him. He was sometimes confused, and not very clear in his words. I could nearly swear he said he offered Saint Augustine a drink, one morning when it was cold.

This was all threatening to put Mick's own carefully formulated plans into disorder – perhaps wreck them. De Selby was no longer the cool scientist who could be met at an agreed level, steel meeting steel. It seemed that on this night he had behaved like a garrulous, dangerous drunk.

– Did he ask for me?

– Hackett first pointed to his empty glass and then stared moistly at his friend.

– Did he ask for you? he repeated. Wasn't he here to meet you on foot of an appointment made by yourself?

– I know, but when I failed to show up did he suggest any other arrangement? For instance, did he say I might call on him?

– No. He was very vague. One of the reasons why he was so disappointed that tonight's meeting fell through was that there seemed to be no possibility of an alternative meeting.

– The man was blithero.

– No, not so much that. He hinted at an impending great change, his own departure, the dropping of all the enterprise he has had going on in that house of his. Well . . . I don't know but he seemed to have something pretty big planned.

Mick sighed. If Hackett's report were to be taken seriously, the situation had become deplorably fluid and formless. Yet for all that, Mick reckoned he was still one jump ahead. If one were to trust the alchemy of barleycorn, De Selby was possibly by now being helped out of his clothes by Teague McGettigan preparatory to collapsing into bed, clutched in the airless womb of liquor. It would probably be high noon on another day before his senses returned to him, and then only to a comatose wreck. A good forty-eight hours would pass before he was fit for doing or deciding anything. But Mick himself would be at work early next morning.

– Well, Hacket, he said, I'm going to buy a final drink and then depart. Tomorrow morning I have to bring to a conclusion what I did today. Afterwards, I might try to contact De Selby over the weekend.

He did summon a glass of whiskey, a glass of Vichy, and managed to give a laugh.

– Cheer up, Hackett, he beamed, don't let collision with an odd and exceptional man like De Selby depress you or extinguish your natural ebullience. You're not good company when you have a load on your mind. There's no need for any load. Forget all about it.

Hackett smiled a little.

– You must excuse me, he replied, but I always feel a bit frustrated when thrown into the company of a man already full of booze. Seems like fighting with one arm tied behind you.

They clinked glasses and Mick found himself saying something which surprised him almost as much as Hackett.

– Hackett, he said, I have been much more mixed up in this supernatural play-acting than you have. One way or another, it is going to end soon. But I've learnt something – something deep and valuable. First, that there *is* another world, though my glimpses of it have been uncertain and distorted. Second, that I have an immortal soul, which I have been doing nothing to safeguard. Third, that the life I have been living is futile and, indeed, laughable.

Hackett chuckled.

– That is certainly a mouthful.

– The same goes for you, though it is true that you have not been so destitute of purpose as I have been. After all, you have set your heart on winning that snooker tournament.

– Is snooker then sinful?

– No, only meaningless. I'm going to throw up my rotten little job as soon as possible and join the Church.

164

Perhaps it was the earnest tone and serious manner, but Hackett did sit up.

– You're . . . you're blathering out of you, Mick, surely? At *your* age?

– I'm in earnest. This thought has been running at the bottom of my head all along, no matter how busy I was on other matters – running like a tireless, invisible electric motor. God's grace never left me.

– Well, I'll be damned. Do you mean to tell me that if I happened to meet you in a few years, I'll have to lift my hat to you? You know perfectly well that I hardly ever wear a hat.

Mick smiled benignly. Serious as he was, he did not want this occasion to become ponderous or pompous and therefore verging on the ridiculous. An ill-timed laugh can wreck an important thing.

– I can relieve your mind on that, Hackett, he said brightly. You are most unlikely to meet me after I have graduated among the Lord's anointed. In fact it will be impossible.

– Why? Are you going to be a foreign missions man, preaching the Gospel to the niggers in Zanzibar or some such place?

– No. This is one thing I will not half-do. I'm old enough to know my own mind. I intend to join one of the enclosed orders – and the toughest of the lot, if they will have me.

– And who are they when they're at home?

The reformed Order of Cistercians, commonly known as the Trappists . . .

A queer clucking sound came from Hackett, and this developed into a bombastic laugh.

– Hell, hell, he sniggered, I'll buy a final drink on that. Have a whiskey this time. Two, Mrs L, he called. As she moved to obey, Mrs Laverty said:

– It's getting on the time, Mr Hackett.

Hackett was momentarily silent, thoughtful, and paid exactly for the goods. He turned to Mick confidentially as by gesture he proposed his health.

– It is curious how an occasion arises for a toast, and arises inevitably, even if one has despaired of it ever arising. Silly words like fate, or predestination, are used for this process.

– Maybe Providence would be a better word.

– Nearly ten years ago, I composed a very clever poem. I locked it in my mind, determined not to parade it until an occasion arose when it would be miraculously apposite. Do you follow me?

– I think I do.

– I was not concerned whether I amassed an undeserved reputation for extemporization. That didn't bother me at all. I just wanted to clinch the issue, put my trump on somebody else's ace. Get me?

– Sounds to me like vanity.

– Wait! This is the occasion. You say you are going to join the Trappists? Right. It is for that announcement that my poem was written so long ago. Here surely is Destiny nakedly at work! But what a pity we haven't an enormous audience.

– Recite your composition, please, Mick ordered.

The other did so, in a solemn voice, and Mick certainly laughed at the end of it. A little bit bawdy perhaps, but not dirty.

There was a young monk of La Trappe
Who contracted a dose of the clap,
*   He said Dominus Vobiscum,*
*   Oh why can't my piss come—*
There's something gone wrong with my . . . tap.

Yes, funny. But Mick's mood was thoughtful as he made his way home that night. He had been wholly serious in what he had said to Hackett. His days as a layman were numbered.

17

Early the next morning Mick was up and about, the rather shadowed mood of the preceding night dissipated and a feeling of satisfaction in his heart, with no clear reason why. He felt his rather messed up mind was clearing, the road ahead plainer.

He put on his good clothes and the breakfast he quickly made was simple – simple as the little job ahead of him that morning. Slipping quietly out at the appointed time, he found the taxi-cab where it should be and the driver Charlie, whom he knew from occasional other jaunts, reading a newspaper. Here was the rich man's Teague McGettigan.

– That's the grand mornin', thank God, Charlie said.

– It is, indeed, Mick replied, getting in beside him, and I wish I was going off down to Arklow for a day's sea-fishing. I'm sure you wouldn't be in the way on a trip like that, Charlie?

– I'm a divil for ling, sir. Matteradamn what I'm after – pollock, mackerel, black sole or even cod – I always get ling. I'm like a trout-fisher that always catches eels and gets his tackle ruined. Vico Road, sir?

– Vico Road, yes. I'll tell you where.

It was nine and not really early in the morning but the trip through Monkstown, Dunleary and Dalkey was as if through habitations still asleep. There was little movement or traffic except for an occasional battered tram-car.

There was not a soul to be seen on the Vico Road. Mick had Charlie drive a fair bit past the target, then go back and stop twelve yards beyond the gap in the railings.

– Just wait here, Charlie, he instructed, and leave the nearside back door open. I have to collect an awkward class of an article from a friend. I won't be long.

– Right, sir.

Mick could see almost at a glance that the cask was where he had left it but he went upward among the trees and sat down on a shoulder of rock. He thought a little artificial delay was called for.

When he did go back he had little trouble in man-handling the cask and achieving the roadside, carrying it before him but on reaching the car he had to dump it heavily to the ground.

– This damn thing is heavy, Charlie, he said, recalling the driver from his newspaper. Could you lift it into the back?

– Certainly, sir.

He did so expertly.

– That's one of them new electric mines, I'll go bail, he said, as both got back into their seats. I seen many like that took out of the sea in the first world war.

– Nothing of the kind, I believe, Mick replied airily, though the man who owns it is in the electrical line. He wants it put away for safety in the Bank of Ireland, out of harm's way, and that's our next stop. He's an inventor.

– Ah yes, Charlie said. That class of man can make millions when the rest of us is scratchin' for coppers.

Later, as Mick entered the Bank of Ireland preceded by Charlie carrying the cask, he felt he was in effect entering the Cistercian Order of Trappists. Perhaps there is a certain monastic quality in banks, a sacred symbolism in money, silver and gold.

– Just leave it on the floor by the side-table there, Charlie, he said, and I think this will pay you for all your trouble.

A friendly cashier readily recognized Mick. Could he see somebody behind the scenes for a moment about a private matter. Not the manager, of course, but some . . . authorized officer? Certainly.

Mr Heffernan, when Mick was shown into his sur-prisingly modern office, was elderly, affable and seemed almost on the point of producing a decanter. When seated and having declined a cigarette, Mick came to the point in what he thought was a brisk manner.

– Mr Heffernan, I am a new customer and a small one. I wanted to enquire about one of the bank's services, of which I've heard. I mean the safe deposit system.

– Yes?

– Is it true that you accept for safe-keeping objects without knowing what they are?

– Yes. Every major bank does.

– But suppose something – a box, say – was in reality an infernal machine? A time-bomb, for instance?

– Well, as Irish institutions go, we're fairly venerable. The Bank of Ireland is still here, eccentric or murderous depositors notwithstanding.

– But . . . one must get rid of the old idea that a time-bomb is necessarily something that ticks. Modern methods, Mr Heffernan, could make a simple thing that looks like an onion, say, to have the explosive power of 10,000 tons of T.N.T.

– Well, from the beginning of the world banking has been a business which entailed risk. That is all I can say. Of course there are certain limitations on our facilities. The physical size of a deposit, for instance, has to conform to certain limits and it must not be a nuisance as, for example, having a bad smell. If you had become fond of a certain old railway engine and bought it, I'm afraid we could not accept it as a deposit. But anything within reason.

– Well, Mr Heffernan, you surprise and relieve me.

They had a messenger bring the cask in. It contained certain small objects produced by an immediate relative in connexion with electronic research; he was a physician in private practice with limited resources for safe storage. The objects were of trifling size *as objects*, and the weight was mostly that of the cask itself. The thing was guaranteed to emit no harmful radiation.

To Mick himself his piece sounded lame but to Mr

Heffernan it was quite satisfactory. After the signing of some papers, the bank had taken over De Selby's treasure and its temporary custodian was once more in the street. And not long after that he was contemplating a glass of cool Vichy water. Wonderful how business people who knew their business could so smoothly do business.

He felt not idle but disoccupied. What would he do with himself until Tuesday, when he had his second meeting with James Joyce at Skerries?

To consider that further and more fully he had a second drink, though he genuinely disagreed with even harmless drinking so early in the day, when it could scarcely be said that the morning had been properly aired. But the cares on him were heavy, and somehow he seemed to be taking on the character of a Cabinet Minister. What did he mean Cabinet Minister? Prime Minister was the more precise term. Policy in several major regards was in his sole charge; he was making – and had made – critical decisions. His resolve to retire from the world personally for the rest of his life was perhaps the most important bit only in so far as it concerned himself and his immortal soul; his recent transaction with the Bank of Ireland concerned the human race, in existence and to come. What of De Selby? To kill him would be gravely sinful but a middle and less brutal course came to mind, one which no doubt betrayed his academic mould of thought. He would spend the vacant weekend committing precisely and temperately to paper the facts concerning De Selby, his chemical work and diabolical scheme, and the action which had been taken, right up to that morning. *And that document he would hand over to the abbot of the Trappist house he joined*, thus passing to an older and wiser head the decision on De Selby's personal future and the fate of the ghastly paraphernalia which no doubt littered the workroom of 'Lawnmower'.

One other thing: the matter of letting Mary know that he had, so to speak, no use for her washing. A letter would be unthinkable and cowardly, and anyway it was desirable to emphasize that it was an austere, enclosed order – not another woman – that had induced him to change his mind so drastically. On Monday or Tuesday he would ask her to meet him in the evening at the Colza Hotel. That spot was pleasantly remote for a heady showdown, if there was to be one, and it was always possible that Hackett might be there.

By then his second investigation of Joyce would be over and perhaps a decision arrived at as to what, if anything, to do about that strange man. To attend to him, and to Mary and Hackett as well, was a grandiose programme for one evening.

18

During his train journey to Skerries on Tuesday evening his mood was peaceable: resigned might be a fairer word. *Quisque faber fortunae suae*, the tag says – everybody makes his own mess. Still, he did not think this outlook applicable. He was conscious of a pervasive ambiguity: sometimes he seemed to be dictating events with deific authority, at other times he saw himself the plaything of implacable forces. On this particular trip he felt he must await an exposition of Joyce by himself, and take him at his face value. Joyce had already whetted curiosity by disclosing that he was still working on a book, unnamed, content unhinted at. He could be an impostor, or a unique case of physical resemblance. Yet his appearance was authentic, and clearly he had lived on the European continent. Really, he could not be classed as one of Mick's problems but rather an interesting distraction for one now practised in interfering in the affairs of others.

Very properly, Mick had not given his own private or business address, and it could not be said that he knew anything embarrassing.

The hotel was a simple establishment, with no bar, but an old man, nondescript in manner and dress to the point of giving no sign whether he was the boots or the proprietor, guided Mick down a hallway to 'the drawing-room where gents takes a drink'. It was an ill-lit room, small, linoleum on the floor, a few small tables with chairs here and there, and in the grate a flickering fire. Mick was alone and agreed with his host that it was a poor evening for that time of the year, and then ordered a small sherry.

– I'm expecting a friend, he added.

But Joyce was punctual. He came in noiselessly, very soberly attired, quiet, calm, a small black hat surmounting his small ascetic features, in his hand a stout walking stick. He sat down after a slight bow.

– I took the liberty of ordering something on the way in, he said, smiling slightly, because we in the trade like to save each other's feet. I hope you are A.I?

Mick laughed easily.

– Excellent, he said. That walk from the station is a tonic in itself. Here's your drink, and I'm paying for it.

Joyce did not reply, having commenced preparing to light a small black cigar.

– I am a little bit flustered, he said finally. You seem to have many connections in this country. I envy you. I know a few people – but friends? Ah!

– Perhaps you are by nature the more solitary type of man, Mick suggested. Maybe company in general doesn't agree with you. Personally, I find interesting people very scarce, and bores to be met everywhere.

He seemed to nod in the gloom.

– One of the great drawbacks of Ireland, he said, is that there are too many Irish here. You understand me? I know it is natural and to be expected, like having wild animals in the zoo. But it's unnerving for one who has been away in the mishmash that is Europe today.

Here he had led Mick to the scene of his enquiry, so to speak. Mick's voice was low, soothing:

– Mr Joyce, I have great respect for you and it would be an honour to be of service to you. I am a bit confused by your eminence as an author and your presence in this part of the world. Would you give me a little information about yourself – in strict confidence, of course.

Joyce nodded as if without guile.

– I will, of course. There is nothing much to tell you. The past is simple enough. The future is what I find remote and difficult.

– I see. Were you expelled from Switzerland by the Hitler people?

– No, France. My wife and family were part of a mass of people fleeing before that terror. My passport was British. I knew I would be arrested, probably murdered.

– What happened to your family?

– I can't say. We got separated.

– Are they dead?

– I know very little except that my son is safe. It was all chaos, bedlam. Trains broke down, lines were damaged. It was improvisation everywhere. A lift in a lorry, perhaps, or stumbling across fields, or holding up for a day or two in a barn. There were soldiers and guerillas and cut-throats roaming the land on all sides. By the Lord God it was not funny. Fortunately the real country folk were recognizable – brave, simple people. Fortunately I could speak French properly.

– And what exactly was your destination?

He paused.

– Well, first, he explained, I wanted to get away from contact with those Germans. My second idea was to get to America. America hadn't entered the war at that time. But any sort of major movement was very difficult. There were spies, saboteurs and thugs of every description high and low. The simplest questions of even food and drink were difficult.

– Yes, war is calamitous.

– I wouldn't dignify that French shambles with the word war. And the black market? Heavens!

– What happened?

– I got to London first. The atmosphere of nerves there was terrible. I didn't feel safe.

Mick nodded.

– I remember they hanged your namesake – the broadcaster Joyce.

– Yes. I thought I'd be better off here. I managed to sneak across in a small freighter. Thank God I can still pass for an Irishman.

– What about your family?

– I'm having confidential enquiries made through a friend, and I know my son is safe. Of course I can't risk making enquiries direct.

The conversation was fair enough but not much to Mick's purpose. Was this James Joyce, the Dublin writer of international name? Or was it somebody masquerading, possibly genuinely deranged through suffering? The old, nagging doubt was still there.

– Mr Joyce, tell me about the writing of *Ulysses*.

He turned with a start.

– I have heard more than enough about that dirty book, that collection of smut, but do not be heard saying that I had anything to do with it. Faith now, you must be careful about that. As a matter of fact, I have put my name only to one little book in which I was concerned.

– And what was that?

– Ah, it's a long time ago. Oliver Gogarty and I, when we were in touch, worked together on some short stories. Simple stories: Dublin characterizations you might call them. Yes, they did have some little merit, I think. The world was settled then . . .

– Did you find that sort of association with Gogarty easy?

Joyce chuckled softly.

– The man had talent, he said, but of a widely spread out kind. He was primarily a talker and, up to a point, his talk improved with drink. He was a drunkard, but not habitually. He was too clever for that.

– Well, you were friends?

– Yes, you could say that, I suppose. But Gogarty could have a scurrilous and blasphemous tongue and that didn't suit me, I needn't tell you.

– Was this collaboration genuinely fifty-fifty?

– No. I did the real work, tried to get back into the soul of the people. Gogarty was all for window-dressing, smart stuff, almost Castle cavorting – things not in character. Oh, we had several quarrels, I can tell you.

– What did you call the book?

– We called it *Dubliners*. At the last moment Gogarty wouldn't let his name go on the title page. Said it would ruin his name as a doctor. It didn't matter, because no publisher could be found for years.

– Very interesting. But what else have you written, mainly?

Joyce quietly attended to the ash of his cigar.

– So far as print is concerned, mostly pamphlets for the Catholic Truth Society of Ireland. I am sure you know what I mean – those little tracts that can be had from a stand inside the door of any church; on marriage, the sacrament of penance, humility, the dangers of alcohol.

Mick stared.

– You surprise me.

– Now and again, of course, I attempted something more ambitious. In 1926 I had a biographical piece on Saint Cyril, Apostle of the Slavs, published in *Studies*, the Irish Jesuit quarterly. Under an assumed name, of course.

– Yes. But *Ulysses*?

There was a low sound of impatience in the gloom.

– I don't want to talk about that exploit. I took the idea to be a sort of practical joke but didn't know enough about it to suspect it might seriously injure my name. It began with an American lady in Paris by the name of Sylvia Beach. I know it's a horrible phrase, I detest it, but the truth is that she fell in love with me. Fancy that!

He smiled bleakly.

– She had a bookshop which I often visited in connexion with a plan to translate and decontaminate great French literature so that it could be an inspiration to the Irish, besotted with Dickens, Cardinal Newman, Walter Scott and Kickham. My eye had a broad range – Pascal and Descartes, Rimbaud, de Musset, Verlaine, Balzac, even that holy Franciscan, Benedictine and medical man, Rabelais . . . !

– Interesting. But *Ulysses*?

– Curious thing about Baudelaire and Mallarmé – both were obsessed with Edgar Allen Poe.

– How did Miss Beach express her love for you?

– Ah-ha! Who is Sylvia? She swore to me that she'd make me famous. She didn't at the beginning say how, and anyhow I took it all patiently as childish talk. But her plot was to have this thing named *Ulysses* concocted, secretly circulated and have the authorship ascribed to me. Of course at first I didn't take the mad scheme seriously.

– But how did the thing progress?

– I was shown bits of it in typescript. Artificial and laborious stuff, I thought. I just couldn't take much interest in it, even as a joke by amateurs. I was immersed in those days in what was intrinsically good behind the bad in Scaliger, Voltaire, Montaigne, and even that queer man Villon. But how well-attuned they were, I thought, to the educated Irish mind. Ah, yes. Of course it wasn't Sylvia Beach who showed me those extracts.

– Who was it?

– Various low, dirty-minded ruffians who had been paid to put this material together. Muck-rakers, obscene poets, carnal pimps, sodomous sycophants, pedlars of the coloured lusts of fallen humanity. Please don't ask me for names.

Mick pondered it all, in wonder.

– Mr Joyce, how did you live in all those years?

– Teaching languages, mostly English, and giving grinds. I used to hang around the Sorbonne. Meals were easy enough to scrounge there, anyway.

– Did the Catholic Truth Society pay you for those booklets you wrote?

– Not at all. Why should they?

– Tell me more about *Ulysses*.

– I paid very little attention to it until one day I was given a piece from it about some woman in bed thinking the dirtiest thoughts that ever came into the human head. Pornography and filth and literary vomit, enough to make even a black-guard of a Dublin cabman blush. I blessed myself and put the thing in the fire.

– Well was the complete *Ulysses*, do you think, ever pub-lished?

– I certainly hope not.

Mick paused for a few seconds and pressed the bell for service. What would he say? Frankness in return seemed called for.

– Mr Joyce, he said solemnly, I can tell you that you have been out of touch with things for a long time. The book *Ulysses* was published in Paris in 1922, with your name on the title page. And it was considered a great book.

– God forgive you. Are you fooling me? I am getting on in years. Remember that.

Mick patted his sleeve, and signalled to a server to bring more drinks.

– It was roughly received originally but it has since been published everywhere, including America. Dozens – literally dozens – of distinguished American critics have written treatises on it. Books have even been written about yourself and your methods. And all the copyright money on *Ulysses* must have accrued to your credit. The difficulty of the

177

various publishers is simply that they don't know where you are.

– May the angels of God defend us!

– You're a strange man, Mr Joyce. Bowsies who write trash and are as proud as punch of it are ten a penny. You have your name on a great book, you are ashamed of your life, and ask God's pardon. Well, well, well. I am going out for a moment to relieve myself. I feel that's about the perfect thing to do.

– How dare you impute smutty writings to me?

Mick got up a bit brusquely and went out for the purpose stated, but was disturbed. His bluff, if that was the right name for it, had hardly succeeded. Joyce was serious in his denial, and apparently had never seen the book *Ulysses*. What new line should now be taken?

When he returned and sat down Joyce quickly spoke in a low and serious tone.

– Look here, I hope you don't mind if we change the subject, he said. I spoke of the importance for me of the future. I mean that. I want you to help me.

– I've already said it would be a pleasure.

– Well, you have heard of Late Vocations. I may not be worthy but I want to join the Jesuits.

– *What*? Well . . . !

The shock in Mick's voice was of a rasping kind. Into his mind came that other book, *Portrait of the Artist.* Here had been renunciation of family, faith, even birthland, and that promise of silence, exile and cunning. What did there seem to be here? The garrulous, the repatriate, the ingenuous? Yet was not even a man of genius entitled to change his mind? And what matter if that mind showed signs of unbalance, and memory evidence of decay? The ambition to join the Church's most intellectual of Orders was certainly an enormous surprise, perhaps not to be taken absolutely seriously. Still, he had custody of his immortal soul and who was he, Mick, himself on the brink of the holy prison of the Trap-

178

pists, to question his wish to take part in the religious life? He might not be taken, of course, by reason of the scandalous literary works attributed to him, or even by reason of age, but that decision was one for Father Provincial of the Society of Jesus, not for Mick.

– My French Plan, if I may call it that, Joyce continued, I could defer until I had the seclusion of the Order. Curious, I have many notes on the *good* and *decorous* things written by those three scoundrels who otherwise dealt in blood – Marat, Robespierre and Danton. Strange . . . like lilies sprouting on a heap of ordure.

Mick drank thoughtfully, arranging his thoughts into wise words.

– Mr Joyce, he said, I believe it takes fourteen years to make a Jesuit Father. That's a long time. You could become a medical doctor in far less than that.

– If God spares me, I would be a postulant even if it took me twenty years. Of what account are those trumpery years in this vale of tears? Do you know any Jesuits personally?

– I do. I know at least one, a Father Cobble, in Leeson Street. He's an Englishman but quite intelligent.

– Ah, excellent. Will you introduce me?

– I will of course. Naturally, that is about all I could do. I mean, Church matters are for the Church to decide. If I were to try to sort of . . . interfere or use pressure, I would be very soon told to mind my own business.

– I quite understand that. All I ask for is a quiet talk with a Jesuit Father after I've been sponsored by some responsible, respectable person like yourself. Leave the rest to him, me and God.

His tone seemed pleased, and in the gloom he gave the impression of smiling.

– Well, I'm glad our little talk is going the right way, Mick said.

– Yes, he murmured. I've just been thinking in recent days of my schooldays at Clongowes Wood College. Of course it's very silly but suppose I were to become a Jesuit as planned, is it not at least possible – *possible*, I repeat – that I would in my old age be appointed Rector of Clongowes? Could it not happen?

– Of course it could.

Joyce's fingers were at his glass of Martini, playing absently. His mind was at grips with another matter.

– I must be candid here, and careful. You might say that I have more than one good motive for wishing to become a Jesuit Father. I wish to reform, first the Society, and then through the Society the Church. Error has crept in ... corrupt beliefs ... certain shameless superstitions ... rash presumptions which have no sanction within the word of the Scriptures.

Mick frowned, considering this.

– Questions of dogma, you mean? These can be involved matters.

– Straightforward attention to the word of God, Joyce rejoined, will confound all Satanic quibble. Do you know the Hebrew language?

– I'm afraid I do not.

– Ah, too few people do. The word *ruach* is most important. It means a breath or a blowing. *Spiritus* we call it in Latin. The Greek word is *pneuma*. You see the train of meaning we have here? All these words mean life. Life, and breath of life. God's breath in man.

– Do these words mean the same thing?

– No. The Hebrew *ruach* denoted only the Divine Being, anterior to man. Later it came to mean the inflammation, so to speak, of created man by the breath of God.

– I find that not very clear.

– Well ... one needs experience in trying to grasp celestial concepts through earthly words. This word *ruach* latterly means, not the immanent energy of God but His transcendent energy in imparting the divine content to men.

– You mean that man is part-God?

– Even the ancient pre-Christian Greeks used *pneuma* to denote the limitless and all-powerful personality of God, and man's bodily senses are due to the immanence of that *pneuma*. God wills that man have a transfusion of His *pneuma*.

– Well . . . I don't suppose anybody would question that. What you call *pneuma* is what distinguishes man from the brute?

– As you will, but it is wrong to say that man's possession, charismatically, of *ruach* or *pneuma* makes him part-God. God is of two Persons, the Father and the Son. They subsist in hypostasis. That is quite clear from mention of both Divine Persons in the New Testament. What I particularly call your attention to is the Holy Spirit – the Holy Ghost, to use the more common title.

– And what about the Holy Spirit?

– The Holy Spirit was the invention of the more reckless of the early Fathers. We have here a confusion of thought and language. Those poor ignorant men associated *pneuma* with what they called the working of the Holy Spirit, whereas it is merely an exudation of God the Father. It is an activity of the existing God, and it is a woeful and shameful error to identify in it a hypostatic Third Person. Abominable nonsense!

Mick picked up his glass and gazed into it in dismay.

– Then you don't believe in the Holy Ghost, Mr Joyce?

– There is not a word about the Holy Ghost or the Trinity in the New Testament.

– I am not . . . much experienced in Biblical studies.

Joyce's low grunt was not ill-natured.

– Of course you're not, because you were reared a Catholic. Neither are the Catholic clergy. Those ancient disputants, rhetoricians, theologizers who are collectively called the Early Fathers were buggers for getting ideas into their heads and then assuming that God directly inspired those ideas. In trying to wind up the Arian controversy, the Council of

Alexandria in 362, having asserted the equality in nature of the Son with the Father, went on to announce the transfer of a third hypostasis to the Holy Spirit. Without saying boo, or debating the matter at all! Holy poky but wouldn't you think they'd have a little sense?

– I always understood that God was of three Divine Persons.

– Well you didn't get up early enough in the morning, my lad. The Holy Ghost was not officially invented until the Council of Constantinople in 381.

Mick fingered his jaws.

– Goodness, he said. I wonder what the Holy Ghost Fathers would think of that?

Joyce noisily rapped his glass and murmured to the server who appeared and took them away. Then he drew expansively at his cigar.

– One thing you *do* know, he asked – the Nicene Creed?

– Sure everybody knows that.

– Yes. The Father and the Son were meticulously defined at the Council of Nicaea, and the Holy Spirit hardly mentioned. Augustine was a severe burden on the early Church, and Tertullian split it wide open. He insisted that the Holy Spirit was derived from the Father *and* the son – *quoque*, you know. The Eastern Church would have nothing to do with such a doctrinal aberration. Schism!

Joyce paid for two new drinks then sat down. His voice had been lively, as if joyous in disputation. Mick's own mind had been awakened sharply by mention of Augustine, and he struggled to get into words a rather remote idea which was forming. He sampled his sherry.

– That word *pneuma*, Mr Joyce . . . ?

– Yes?

– Well, you remember my friend De Selby, whom I mentioned to you?

– I do indeed. Dalkey.

– I told you he was a physicist . . . a theologian also.

182

– Yes. Fascinating mixture but not incongruous, mind you.

– You will probably laugh in my face if I told you to believe that I met Saint Augustine in the company of De Selby.

Joyce's cigar glowed dimly.

– Faith, now – *laugh?* Certainly not. There are conditions . . . opiates . . . gases – many ways of confuting weak human reason.

– Thank you, Mr Joyce. I'll talk about the Augustine affair another time, but the circumstance of this encounter involved the operation of a formula whereby De Selby claims to be able to stop the flow of time, or reverse it.

– Well, it is a big claim.

– It is. But the phrase he used to describe his work was 'pneumatic chemistry'. You see? That world *pneuma* again.

– Indeed yes. Life, breath, eternity, recall of the past. I must think about this man De Selby.

– I'm glad you are so serious and reasonable. *Pneuma* in its divine aspect seems to have been concerned somehow in the manifestation of Saint Augustine.

– One must not be astonished at a thing merely because it looks impossible.

Mick's thought was occupied with another encounter disclosing a situation which, if not impossible, was certainly unlikely.

– Mr Joyce, he said, I have another unusual experience which seems to have involved this *pneuma* also.

– Oh, I don't wonder. It's a big subject. We call it pneumatology.

– Yes. I know a Sergeant Fottrell, also of Dalkey. He has an involved theory about the danger of riding bicycles, even if they are fitted with pneumatic tyres.

– Ah, bicycles? I never had any love for those machines. The old Dublin cab was my father's first choice for getting around.

– Well, the sergeant thinks that, *pneuma* in the tyres or not, the rider gets a severe jolting and that there is an exchange or interfusion of bicycle atoms and human atoms.

Joyce quietly drank.

– Well . . . I would not reject the possibility outright. The *pneuma* there might be preserving life, in the sense of preserving the physical integrity of the rider. Half an hour in a laboratory is a thing that would help us here. The interchange of cells of human tissue with elements of metal would seem a surprising occurrence but of course that is merely a rational objection.

– All right. In any case the sergeant had no doubt of it. He personally knew men whose *jobs* entailed much cycling every day and he regarded some of them as more bicycle than man.

Joyce chuckled dimly.

– There we have a choice. Psychical research or cycle research. I prefer the psychical. Ah, indeed . . . my own little troubles are more complicated than the sergeant's. I have to get into the Jesuits, you might say, to clear the Holy Ghost out of the Godhead and out of the Catholic Church.

There was a silence. Mick's business seemed almost at an end. It had been a short evening, yet Joyce's disclosures about himself, past and present, had not been inconsiderable. Joyce moved in his chair.

– Tell me, he said, how soon could I see Father Cobble?

– How soon? Well, as soon as you like, I suppose. These men are usually accessible enough at any time.

– What about tomorrow?

– Goodness!

– You see, I have three days off from work just now – from work as a curate. Could we strike the iron while it's hot?

Mick pondered this urge for action. All he could think about it was – why not?

– Well, I have an appointment at Dalkey tomorrow night. But provided I could meet you somewhere in town about half-six or so, I suppose we could go along and meet Father

Cobble. I could telephone him during the day and make the appointment.

– Excellent. Excellent.

– What time would you say for a meeting? The place I suggest is outside St Vincent's Hospital, on the Green. But at what time?

– Yes. I know the hospital. Would seven in the evening suit?

Mick agreed with this: it would fit neatly into his schedule. They fell silent, finishing their drinks. Was there anything else of a semi-private nature to be asked, Mick wondered, for there would be very little opportunity for confidence the following day. Yes, there was: one thing.

– Mr Joyce, he said, I know the subject displeases you but I must return briefly to that work *Ulysses*. Do you mind?

– No, no, but it's just a boring, dirty subject.

– I take it you have no literary agent?

– What would I have the like of that for?

– Well, I mean—

– Do you think the Catholic Truth Society are commercial publishers, on the make?

– Never mind. Would you appoint me your literary agent?

– Call yourself that by all means if it pleases you, I can't imagine why.

– Well, it's like this. Notwithstanding your ignorance, there may be money lying to your credit from the sales of *Ulysses* in the accounts of publishers. There may be several thousands of pounds there. There is no reason why you should not claim money which is your due – no reason that I should not claim it on your behalf.

– You would probably be offended if I were to say that you suffer from an obsession, from an excited imagination.

Mick laughed lightly to put him at ease.

– You ought to know, he said, that a person who seems to get a bit light-headed should be humoured.

– Well, yes. . . flighty children should be treated that way.

It saves trouble. But you're no child, even if the bottle is no stranger to you.

Both of them relaxed.

– There can be no harm in me, as your agent, making enquiries. Now can there?

– There certainly would appear to be no breach of the moral law involved, and that's a sure fire. The only thing you must never reveal is my address – particularly not to any of those lascivious pornographic blackguards.

Mick drank audibly.

– Perhaps you may have something else to say, he said mildly, if it turns out that there is a sum of £8000 due on foot of *Ulysses*.

Joyce's voice, when it came, was low and strained.

– What would *I* do with £8000? he demanded – a man who is tomorrow taking the first step to join the Jesuit Order?

– As I think I reminded you before, they call it Society, not Order. And I can tell you this. If they take you, they take you as you are, poor or rich. The founder Loyola was a nobleman, remember that. And another thing . . .

– What?

– If sundry scheming ruffians in Paris or elsewhere imputed to you matter you did not write and sought to besmear your good name, would it not look like Divine Providence if their base handiwork were to turn out to do you immense corporal good?

Joyce smoked testily.

– But I tell you I don't want or need money.

– Maybe you do. The Jesuits have a wide choice. It may be that they are not particularly fond of paupers.

The silence which followed possibly meant that Joyce was acknowledging a quite new idea. He spoke at last.

– All right. If £8000 was in fact earned by that horrible book you mentioned, and can be lawfully got, every penny of it will go to the Jesuits except five pounds, which I will devote to the Holy Souls.

They parted soon after, Mick strolling towards the station, well enough at ease.

He doubted whether the Jesuits would accept a man of his age, other questions apart. Perhaps some other Order would take him as a Brother. Any Order, he hastily warned himself, except the Trappists. He must never mention that community in Joyce's presence.

19

Coming in through the Green towards the hospital, Mick's eye penetrated the tracery of shrubs and iron railings. Yes, Joyce was standing there, and Mick paused to appraise him soberly in the wan evening sunlight before he knew he was observed. He was by now no stranger, yet in his solitary standing there he was still a bit surprising. He looked a mature man, at ease, iron-grey hair showing from a small hat, symbol of life's slow ebb-tide: also experience, wisdom and – who knows? – adversity. He was neat in person, clean, and had a walking stick. A dandy? No. The carriage of his head in the fuss of traffic and passing people gave notice that his eyesight was uncertain. If a stranger were to try to classify Joyce socially, he would probably put him down as a scholarly type – a mathematician, perhaps, or a tired senior civil servant; certainly not a writer, still less a great writer gone (as was supposed) queer in the head. Mick did not doubt, incidentally, that he had in fact written those pamphlets for the Catholic Truth Society, for mimicry and mockery were usually among the skills of the intellectually gifted; indeed, it was generally true that precision in playing a role ordained by morbid cerebral hypostasis is characteristic of most persons troubled in the mind. Who has not met and admired with pity the authentic attitude, speech and mannerisms of a Napoleon, a Shelley, even a Michelangelo?

Yet the same Joyce must have been somehow connected with the writing of *Ulysses* and *Finnegans Wake*, certainly far more than the probably hallucinatory attributions of authorship by Sylvia Beach. There was a possibility that both books were the monumental labours of several uniquely gifted minds, but a central, unifying mind seemed inescapable. It was not the false imputations of authorship which drove Joyce askew but rather the lonely exertion of keeping pace with a contrived reputation was what finally put the delicate poise of his head out of balance. Yet of Joyce one cheerful thing could be said – there was no harm in him. He was not even a nuisance, and certainly no danger to himself or others. His desire to become a Catholic priest (and alas, in one of the more discerning Orders) was, of course, fanciful; but it would be a great charity if the Jesuits took him. In their several houses about Dublin and throughout Ireland (to go no further) there was surely some nook, some neat little sinecure where he might come to peace. Again there came to mind that slogan of theirs – *ad majorem Dei gloriam*. It was their duty to help one, now fallen, whom they had once undertaken to educate. Joyce's confusion about *Finnegans Wake* was absolute and it was desirable, Mick reflected, that his pattern of thought should be steered completely away from books and writing. He must try to do that and also stress the impossibility (one thing which apparently Joyce himself had recognized) of the name James Joyce in conversations with the clergy. The name most commonplace throughout all Dublin and Wicklow was Byrne, pronounced Burn. He was a retired teacher named James Byrne, with experience on the continent. And was this not a bright thought coming to Mick just then in the Green? He had already mentioned that name to Father Cobble on the telephone.

He crossed the street and had to touch Joyce's arm before he turned in recognition.

– Ah, he said, good evening. That was a nice dry day.

– It was, Mick replied, and I hope we will have a successful twilight, if you know what I mean. We have a little time in hand before meeting Father Cobble.

Joyce smiled bleakly.

– I hope Father Cobble won't be a severe sort of holy man, he ventured.

– No, Mick replied. I told you he is an Englishman, and the only danger is that he may be stupid.

He took Joyce by the arm and guided him round the corner into Leeson Street.

– I want to mark your card, he said, on a few simple matters. We could talk across in the Green but a brief session in here in Grogan's might be better.

They were entering a public house when Joyce's tentative manner showed his surprise.

– Look, he said, there is nothing better I'd like than a small drink but to go for an interview concerning God's work with alcohol on the breath – surely that would be rash?

Mick pushed him to a seat in the snug and pressed a bell.

– First, he replied, Father Cobble himself, like most Jesuits, is not a bit puzzled about what to do when he finds a glass of malt in his hand. Secondly, we are going to have a few gins, not whiskey. Gin does not smell, or so they say. But it helps the tongue and the imagination. For myself, I am joining you in a drink against my will because I intend to give it up entirely, probably from today.

He ordered two glasses, with tonic water.

Joyce acquiesced in silence but gave the impression that he had never heard of gin. Perhaps Geneva would have been a better name.

– Now listen, Mick said briskly, your name from now on is James Byrne. *Your name is James Byrne.* Have you got that? Can you remember that name?

189

Joyce nodded.

– Byrne is a collateral name on my mother's side. Of course I can remember it. James Byrne.

He drank deeply, deceived by the tonic water, and nodded firmly.

– Yes, my name is James Byrne.

He drank again, still nodding, pressed the bell and ordered another round. Mick was slightly nervous.

– Do not take this harmless dram too fast, he counselled. Furthermore, you are a retired teacher, with some experience in France.

– Exactly. I could meet any cross-questioning you like on that point.

He seemed calm, confident, even happy. He was more responsive than usual and Mick honestly felt that he would impress a very neutral person like Father Cobble. Would there be any question about his birth certificate? Possibly, but the matter could be shelved temporarily.

They were respectable enough when they knocked on the large, discreet door of the big house at 35, Lower Leeson Street. An unkempt and ill-spoken youth opened it and showed them off the hall into a waiting-room which was (Mick thought) tawdry, gloomy and indeed a bit dirty. Saintliness and cleanliness were not always kin, he reflected, but there was no reason why that boy, who had now departed in search of Father Cobble, had not washed himself that day and cleaned himself up.

– I discern the authentic note of austerity here, Joyce remarked pleasantly.

– Yes, Mick concurred. Not far removed from the desert of ancient times. I can console you by telling you that the Fathers eat very well here and have red wine with dinner.

Joyce smiled knowingly.

– But I suppose it is not compulsory. In my own days in France I avoided table wines. It is a stupid French delusion that safe drinking-water is impossible to get.

The door had opened silently and there before them stood Father Cobble. Mick felt he had just dined, and was in good humour.

— Well, he said, advancing with both hands outstretched, welcome to our humble house.

There was some perfunctory handshaking, and the priest sat down.

— Father Cobble, Mick said, this is my friend James Byrne. He spent many years teaching abroad but he has now, so to speak, returned to the fold.

— Ah, Mr Byrne, it is a pleasure.

— My job here, Father, Mick added, is just to make this introduction and then be off with myself. James just wants to have a little chat with you.

— Of course. We people here are servants and not a bit ashamed to give ourselves that title. We give advice only for the asking ... He paused and chuckled. Sometimes even without the asking.

— You are very kind, Father, Joyce said. You make me feel at home. You put me at my ease.

There was a pause as if all were waiting for one of them to say something which would at least hint at the purpose of the visit. Finally Father Cobble expertly opened a doorway.

— If it is a spiritual matter you are troubled about, Mr Byrne, he said, I will of course see you alone.

— I am departing anyway, Mick said hastily.

— Do you mean Confession? Joyce asked nervously. Lord no, it's not that. Thank God, I'm in no need of that at all. But it is true that my problem is, well, spiritual.

Father Cobble nodded encouragingly.

— You see, Father, Mick ventured, Mr Byrne wants to enter your house. He knocks at the door.

Here Joyce nodded eagerly.

— Oh well ... I see, Father Cobble said, clearly a bit puzzled.

– He is by no means as old as he looks, Mick added help-fully.

Father Cobble studied his delicate hands.

– Well, the position is roughly this, he explained. Leaving aside ecclesiastical work proper, the community here is responsible for all its own intellectual work such as literary matters, teaching, and the Society's internal administrative tasks, national and international. We are self-sufficient, almost – if I dare say so – almost on the lines of the primitive Church. To look after our simple temporal needs, we take in boys from institutions, boys usually a bit defective mentally but likely to benefit and improve in surroundings like these. And, gentlemen, I make my own bed.

Joyce gestured slightly, momentarily incoherent.

– Father, he said faintly, it is not that I am destitute or anything like that. I have quite a reasonable job in the catering business. It's just that I'm spiritually . . . at sea. I want to serve the Almighty deliberately and directly. I want to come into one of the Society's houses and . . . well, work there.

– I see, Father Cobble said kindly. Yes. But within our rules it is not very easy to fit in a man like you, Mr Byrne. I will have a word with Father Baldwin of Rathfarnham Castle, our other house, and I'll possibly also talk to Milltown Park. We are rather crude people, Mr Byrne. Frankly, we don't go in for horticulture.

Joyce and Mick glanced at each other.

– Thank God we're never far away from a community of good nuns who gladly supply beautiful flowers for the altar.

– In fact, Father, Mick interposed, that sort of thing was not in Mr Byrne's mind at all.

– Well, take Rathfarnham Castle, the good priest continued. There is always a fair amount of weeding and that sort of thing to be done but I know the Rector encourages the Fathers to lend a hand there, for fresh air is as good for the clergy as it is for their flocks. But real gardening is a different cup of tea. Are you an experienced gardener, Mr Byrne?

Mick noticed Joyce coloured slightly under his natural pallor.

– Indeed and I am not, he said loudly.

– I know they have a full-time gardener there, though nowadays he's getting a bit old. But have you other manual qualifications or skills, Mr Byrne? French polishing, carpentry, book-binding . . . ?

– No, Joyce said curtly.

– The care of brasswork?

– No.

Father Cobble smiled tolerantly.

– Well now, Mr Byrne, he said, in the words of soldier, we're not beaten yet. I'll be perfectly honest and tell you that there's one thing which has plagued the Society in all its houses in this country . . .

– Not competition from the Christian Brothers? Mick asked, grinning.

– Ah no. Something much nearer home. I mean the Fathers' underclothes.

– Dear goodness, Joyce said.

– We need not theorize, Father Cobble continued in his mild manner, as to why the Almighty distributed certain skills and crafts as between the sexes. The plain fact is that knitting and sewing and needlework are uniquely the accomplishments of women. The Fathers' underclothes are perpetually in a state of near-collapse, yet our rules prohibit the employment of women here, even in the most menial tasks. That, gentlemen, is a glimpse of the enclosed religious life. Just now my own semmet would make you laugh. Full of holes.

Joyce seemed at sea, embarrassed.

– But Father, surely the nuns could help – even, I mean, as an act of charity?

– No, no, Mr Byrne, our rules do not permit any association of that kind in the domestic sphere. Beautiful flowers for the altar – ah, certainly.

– But, Father, Mick interposed, couldn't, say, old boys from the Jesuit colleges help in a thing like that? Bring stuff home, I mean. After all, they have wives and daughters.

– And mothers and sisters, Joyce added.

Father Cobble smiled remotely.

– The Society of Jesus, gentlemen, has also its dignity.

All paused at this solemnity.

– But good heavens, Father, you must have some way of working—

– If we only knew, Father Cobble observed, why sweat is so corrosive, we would be perhaps getting somewhere. Upon my word my semmet is *rotted*.

Mick's face clouded in some despair.

– But what *do* you do?

– Well, nearly all the Fathers know how to darn socks. Father d'Arbois, a Frenchman here, makes heroic attempts with the underclothes, and one of our houseboys is also quite promising. But thank God there is one bright spot. Father Rector is most generous about renewals. He is very particular about the health of the Fathers. I suspect he has the leg of a floorwalker in Todd Burns.

Joyce, who had been most perplexed, now broke into an easy smile.

– Father Cobble, he said, that household problem may seem formidable but it would not deter myself in the slightest.

– Really, Mr Byrne?

The priest stared at him thoughtfully, and looked towards Mick.

– Do you know, Mr Byrne, he said, I think – forbid that I am being presumptuous – I think you have put an idea into my head. Our sad little situation here obtains equally in our other houses. Not in our Colleges in the country, of course – Clongowes, Mungret, Galway. A matron and staff are provided there but think of our Manresa house at Dollymount, Loyola at Donnybrook, Rathfarnham Castle, Milltown Park. Do you follow me, Mr Byrne? The Fathers' underclothes are in flitters in all those establishments.

Mick stirred uneasily.

– Mr Byrne, Father, he said, is not connected with any of the laundry families or anything like that.

Father Cobble smiled patiently.

– Heaven forbid, he said pleasantly. It is only that I have the embryo of an idea that I think I will put plump and plain before Father Rector.

– And what might that be? Mick asked.

– Quite simple. Just this: that Mr Byrne, having been nominally recruited to our houseboy staff, should be in charge of the maintenance and repair of the Fathers' underclothes in all the Dublin residential establishments.

– Good Lord! Mick gasped.

– To do what he can himself, patiently learning a difficult craft, and to farm out garments to girls of the unfortunate class housed by the good nuns at Donnybrook and Merrion, as God and reason may guide him. Gentlemen . . .

Father Cobble beamed serenely on the visitors.

– Gentlemen, what do you say?

Mick stared ahead of him, stunned, and Joyce seemed unnaturally still in his chair, as if dead. Then his voice was heard, aghast, far off:

– The what was that? Me . . . darn . . . Jesuits' . . . semmets?

Father Cobble looked questioningly from one to the other, himself now slightly puzzled. He had just faced up rather neatly, he thought, to a problem which to them had looked intractable enough. Mick thought furiously in this situation of paralysis. He suddenly stood up.

– Father Cobble, he said seriously, I have to go now, and I'll let myself out. Mr Byrne will explain fully in my absence the sort of work he wishes to embark on. In a word, he wishes to start studies with the object of being ordained a priest . . . and indeed a Jesuit priest.

Father Cobble had also staggered to his feet.

– What was that? *What?* May the Blessed Mother look down on us!

Joyce remained seated, immobile.

– What in heaven's name do you mean? Father Cobble demanded.

Mick fingered his hat and put it on his head.

– Exactly what I said, Father. Goodbye now, take care of yourself, and of Mr Byrne. Goodbye, James. I'll see you later.

It was an inexpressible relief to find himself again in the street, though feelings were confused and there was a stale sense of guilt. Had he cynically made a fool of Joyce? Not deliberately, certainly, but it might have been more prudent to have ignored Dr Crewett's disclosure that Joyce was alive and in Ireland. The latter's mental turmoil had possibly been exacerbated rather than eased. Who could be sure? At all events he was now in hands trained to help, and to give succour in its many forms: he was no longer pitifully helpless, in mid-air. And heretofore ranked as 'problem' in Mick's mind, the tag could now be changed to 'disposed of', if not solved.

What remained? A visit to the Colza Hotel in Dalkey straight away to have it out with Mary, and finally slam closed that draughty door.

As he walked towards a tram, his steps were slow and his face preoccupied.

20

The thoughts in Mick's head seemed to lurch about in the manner of the big tram which was carrying him to Dalkey but those thoughts lacked the familiarity and predestination of the old tramcar.

His outlook was a bit ragged in setting about what should be the careful, conclusive foray in his life. The two preceding episodes had been rough but not unsatisfactory: he had allayed the De Selby menace, possibly forever, and he had brought James Joyce spiritually to a place where more than likely some shadow of the solace he sought would be forthcoming. Even if it was found that he was indeed a head-case, the Fathers would look after him.

Why should he now be vaguely apprehensive about the rest of the night's business? It concerned, for a change, largely himself and his future. He would simply tell Mary firmly, even crudely, that he had no further time for her, and that that was that finally. Memories, or recollections of tenderness long past, was just sentimentality, silly schoolboy inadequacy, like having a dirty nose. He was a grown man, and should behave like one. Why, though, hadn't he ascertained whether the Cistercians had a home in Dublin? It was a stupid omission, for it put him in the position that night of being ready to go but not knowing where to turn. And what about his mother? If he quit his job and entered a monastery, how would she live? That had been decided: with her younger sister who, if far from opulent, had a healthy daughter and ran a boarding-house.

What was needed above all things was calm.

Knowing people and accepting company indiscriminately complicated the already far-from-simple task of living. There might be some truth in the sneer that monks and nuns were merely cowards who ran away from life's challenge, being content unto death to sleep, eat, pray, and mess about with some childishly useless 'work'. Was the monastery just a contrivance for isolation and insulation, not unlike a fever hospital? No, it was God's own house. Notions like that were nefarious in origin. What possible benefit had he derived from, for instance, his association with Hackett? Or, for that matter, with Mary? The one stimulated alcoholism, the other concupiscence. What of the dozens of people of both sexes he knew in the civil service? They were pathetic, futile nobodies, faceless creatures, and – worse – they were bores. Perhaps other people found himself a bore? What matter? Why should he worry about what other people thought? As an intending Trappist, he would have to turn his back on pleasure but that would not be so easy because he knew of practically nothing which could be called pleasure.

As his machine clattered to a final halt, he dimly discerned the Dalkey street below, early lights peeping in a few shops. As he stumbled down the stairs, he realized that he was in a bad temper. Why? Oh, nothing particular – nothing that a good decent drink (not gin) wouldn't fix before he took on Mary in the Colza. At the nearest licensed counter he studied the amber charm of a glass of whiskey and made up his mind once again that he must behave himself. *Finnegans Wake*, though, and all that line of incoherent trash be damned! What was the teaching of the Church on this question of literary depravity? He did not know but perhaps he could find out from one of those little Catholic Truth Society pamphlets, price tuppence.

Gradually an equanimity of mood descended on him. His mission was simple and honourable, his primary object the redemption of his soul. What was wrong with that? Nothing. But the necessary declarations could be made courteously, losing nothing of force for that. Bawling or rude manners impressed nobody, except possibly a member of the brute creation. What if Mary created a scene? It was quite unthinkable. Her attitude of poise, intellectual maturity and sophistication may have been all humbug but one cannot discard a life-long affectation as if it were an old jacket. There would be no scene and as if to register that prediction, he ordered a final glass of what might very remotely be called his pleasure, soon to be spurned forever. The Cistercians? Simple: a glance at a telephone directory on the morrow would locate those saintly men at their best proximity. He murmured to himself a wise Irish proverb: *God's help is nearer than the door.*

When he opened the door of the Colza Hotel, he sensed that he had stumbled on a special silence, sensing also that he himself had been under discussion. Mary and Hackett were alone together at the far end. It was clear from Hackett's lolling attitude and glossy eyes that he had been filling himself with drink for a long time. Mary was not drunk – he had never seen her go any real distance on that path – but her face looked pale and excited. Mrs Laverty was behind the counter, silent, looking strangely chastened. Mick nodded to all in a pleasant but impassive way, sat at the counter and murmured that he would like a whiskey.

– Enter the Prince of Denmark! Hackett said, a thickness in his loud voice.

Mick paid no attention. When he got his drink, he turned towards Mary.

– What sort of a day had you, Mary? he asked. Good, or dull, or just plain unremarkable?

– Oh, just so-so, she replied rather lifelessly.

– The evenings are drawing in, Mrs Laverty said.

– What have you been up to, divil? Hackett rasped.

– I have something to say, Mary . . .

– Is that so, Michael?

Michael! The word stunned him. His name was Mick. Even the ticket checker on the railway called him that, and so did many a barman. To be called Michael – by Mary! Well, well. This was certainly the queer prelude to the play he had composed.

– Did you hear me? Hackett said gruffly, sitting up. Quit this yapping for a few seconds. An explanation is called for. Confront him with the evening paper, Mrs Laverty.

The listless Mrs Laverty transferred the paper from her lap to the counter. The main headline meant nothing to Mick but across two other columns in big letters he read DISASTROUS DALKEY FIRE – Small Mansion Gutted. His startled eyes raced to the smaller print and soon verified that it was indeed De Selby's hide-away. It was understood, the report said, that the owner was in London. The Dunleary brigade had been severely hampered by poor water pressure and the inaccessibility of the conflagration. The building and its contents were totally destroyed and there was even fire damage to some trees. Almost without knowing, Mick swallowed the rest of his drink. Here was a how-do-you-do if there ever was one. Here was he sitting quietly at a counter, the far-seeing genius who had salvaged D.M.P. Lord!

– You might as well tell us all about it. Everybody here, Mary included, knows De Selby. Did he put you up to firing the house? Out with the truth, Mick, for goodness' sake. We're all friends here.

– Wasn't that a terrible thing? Mrs Laverty asked piously and quietly. Pushing his glass across to her, Mick asked when did this happen?

– Very early this morning.

– Tell us what sort of trickery has been going on, Hackett insisted rudely. I know finding out things will be a job for poor Sergeant Fottrell but let's have a few hints. Is this an old-fashioned insurance job?

Mick's reply was blunt.

– Shut up, Hackett. You're a drunken sleeveen.

There must have been real edge on his tone, for utter silence followed, or at least a brief interval filled by nothing but the sound of slobbering by Hackett at his glass. But Mary's penetrating tone came again.

– You said you had something to say?

– Yes.

Why not say it in front of Hackett, even though it was none of his business? Hackett was of no account, though having a witness was no harm.

– Yes, Mary, he said. I have something important to say to you but it's not confidential and I don't mind saying it here.

– You're very snooty tonight whatever you've been up to, Hackett muttered.

– Is that so, Michael, Mary said again, icily. Well, I have something substantial to say to you and I think I'd better say it first. A lady has precedence.

– Aw now, cut out these fireworks, you two, Hackett said. Cut it out.

– Yes, Mary?

– What I wanted to say is that tonight Hackett here has asked me to marry him. I told him I will. We are old friends.

Mick felt limp. He stared, slid off the stool, steadied himself, and then sat up again.

– That's right, Mick, Hackett blabbed, we're old, old friends and we're not getting younger. So we've decided to take the jump and be fluthered ever afterwards. No hard feelings, Mick, but you and Mary weren't engaged. You never gave her a ring.

– That wouldn't matter, Mary interposed.

– We've been going to shows and pubs and dances for weeks and weeks . . . and weeks. One thing about Mary – she's alive. You never suspected that or if you did, you kept the discovery secret.

Mary shook Hackett smartly.

– No need for that sort of talk, she said. His nature is different from yours and that's all. Let's have no clowning here.

– True enough, Hackett said, finishing his drink with a weak flourish. True enough. When you wanted to go out, he stayed at home to make stirabout for his poor mother.

Mick involuntarily again slipped from his stool.

– If you mention my mother again, he snarled, I'll smash your dirty mouth.

Mary frowned.

– Mrs L, Hackett called, give us a new drink on the double – all round. It's ridiculous for people like us to be quarrelling like babbies. All right, Mick, cool down.

Mick got back on his stool.

– What I wanted to say, Mary, he announced slowly, doesn't matter now. It doesn't matter.

Mary, he thought, blanched. It may have been a trick of the light, but her eyes sought the floor. Mick felt strangely touched.

– Tell us something, Hackett said with his greasy friendliness, about that James Joyce of yours if De Selby is barred as a subject of chat.

Mick felt neutralized, if that phrase makes sense. He even mutely accepted Hackett's new drink. What could he say? What *was* there to say?

– Yes, Mary's voice said. Let's talk about something else.

They drank uneasily in silence.

– Joyce, Mick said in the end, wherever he is and however he feels, was in his day a great writer. I'm wondering what sort of a job he would make of the story of Mary and me.

This speech of his own, as he heard it, sounded strange and pathetic. Mary was pale, preoccupied. Hackett was merely drunk. Hackett spoke again.

– Mick, you can keep your Mr Joyce. Know who could write a better book?

– Who?

– Mary here.

– Well, I know she's versatile.

– Ah, that's the word. Versatile.

Then she spoke.

– I don't think that's a story I'd like to try to write. One must write outside oneself. I'm fed up with writers who put a fictional gloss over their own squabbles and troubles. It's a form of conceit, and usually it's very tedious.

There was another considerable pause. Surely they were behaving absurdly – talking about books in a sort of study-circle calm immediately after a nasty flare-up in which personal feelings had been engaged, with the outside possibility of violence. It was artificial, bogus. Mick was beginning to be sorry he'd come, or spoken, or drunk so much. Hackett was now frowning; probably he had lost his way in the maze of his confused thinking. Mary kept her head down, her face a bit averted from Mick. The latter felt that everybody was uneasy. It was Hackett who broke the stillness, and he seemed to be talking mostly to himself.

– Mary, he muttered, let's forget this bargain of ours. We'd good times, but I'm no use. I'm drunk. I'm not your style at all.

She turned to look at him and said nothing.

– That damn fellow over there is all right, Hackett muttered on, and you know that very well. Look at him. He's blushing.

Very likely Mick was. He was upset, and felt a fool. Events seemed to have been perversely pulled inside out inasmuch as he felt he was to blame for making Mary feel like a pig. His ridiculous remedy was to ask Mrs Laverty to dish out another drink all round. He commandeered them, got a tray, and served them personally. His toast was loud:

– To us!

It was silently honoured.

– You didn't mean that, Mary? he murmured.

– No Mick. You're just a bloody fool.

– But the bloody fool you're going to marry?

– I suppose so. I like Hackett here, but not that much.

– Thanks, you cluck, Hackett smiled.

That is as much as need be told. The silence between them on the home-bound tram was mutually known and nursed. What had happened, after all? Nothing much. They had stupidly lost each other, but only for a matter of hours. Mary spoke:

– Mick, what was that awful thing you were going to say tonight?

The question was inevitable, Mick thought, but required care.

– Oh, about my mother, he said. She's getting feebler and has decided to go up to Drogheda and live with her sister.

Mary lightly gripped his wrist.

– Ah, the grand old lady! And the little house? I suppose we'll live there? There's nothing like a roof over your head. It's an old-fashioned idea, but a roof means security – for ourselves and the family.

– The family?

– Yes, Mick. I'm certain I'm going to have a baby.